Contents

Chapter 1 – Introductions

One hears of humidity but when the temperature is 105 degrees does it really make a difference? There are folks who had lived here all their life that might dispute the fact. After all, it is a dry heat. However as he climbed the hill on the highway to the coast the temperature gauge in car dropped and the distant town was more detectable by the mile. The sky was blue and the hills were a beautiful green for the present, fleeting as it is. The car wizzes past "The Spot" and he wonders with abandon why it is significant to him and then he knows in an instant. It must be associated with her. This area is familiar but he doesn't wonder why, in fact what is more surprising is that he has forgotten.

His faded jeans contrast with the black of his shirt, he takes off his hat and still is surprised when there is not a breeze. Is it surprising or appropriate that he is thinking of her, he doesn't know. The car stops and he doesn't know where he is yet. Why does it seem familiar? Was she here? Yet he knows the answer before the question finishes crossing his mind.

This was the first time they spoke. He could envision her brown hair, and his trip back up the trail to help with her pack.

"Do you want help with that?"

"I'm fine"

"I can take it if you want?"

"If you want"

"Would I have asked otherwise?"

Her only response was a motion for him to take it. She watches him take her pack, and as relieved as she is she won't let anyone know. She would have continued, red-faced and puffing along, if he had not insisted. As she walks along carefree, she wonders if anyone else has enjoyed the trip as much, with the freedom and ease she was feeling now. She wonders why he offered to take her pack, surely she looked the weakest and most tired however since she was not used to being noticed, this was maddening. She didn't want to be known as the girl who couldn't make it. She had made it before after all, he was the newbie. Yet as she walked behind him she was very grateful for his help.

Camp was a flurry of activity. Tents, the mandatory scavenge for wood, all in the matter of a couple of hours. She slid into her tent and watched as the other tents go up. The hike had been worth it, but she was so glad they didn't have to repeat it tomorrow. A group started volleyball and she couldn't imagine anyone having the strength after that hike so she just stays where she is. She can see him, bronze in the skin as if a flush from the hike never struck him; he really belonged to this sun. A water bottle later, she was out on the sideline observing the game and a sideways glance caught her eye, but he instantly got back in the game, spiking the ball with an energy she didn't understand, let alone have.
Several times she was asked to join the game but he didn't seem to notice, but why he would, she didn't know.

LOVE HOPES ALL THINGS

Night falls and campfire is raging with the group nestled around on logs and chairs. She is so tiny her pants are short as if she doesn't realize they are too short for her. Why does he notice?

Almost everyone retires; she can hear the fire and the distant talk of those around it from her tent. She snuggles in her sleeping bag to the sound of teenagers flirting and while it sounds so natural she wonders why she doesn't't picture him smiling like he should be. Why does she notice his reaction to her step-sisters flirting? She immediately feels a connection to him, why, because he took her pack? Calling herself silly is the last thing she remembers as she falls asleep.

He awakens to the sound of campfire and the smell of bacon. It is not as hot here and relief is welcoming. He slides into shorts and steps out of the tent to see her pouring herself a cup of coffee.

He can't stand coffee, yet the sight makes him want a cup. Breakfast is eaten and two cups later she watches him finish his breakfast. People are talking about capture the flag already and his focus instantly goes to the surroundings and where he can hide. Teams are created and the game begins, before they know it they are they only two left in the game, him after the flag and her defending it. He watches her at the flag and for a first time there is something beside the flag in his sight. She has been sitting defending the flag, yet the vein in her neck is pulsing as if she had scoured the mountain as he had. After a moments stalemate he realizes he is not alone, another team mate is left and has joined him. She is obviously defeated yet she won't give up. Her eyes dash back and forth and she can't obviously defeat the two but he watches her face and the determination makes him almost wish her the win. However the boyish selfishness in him knows she must go down. His friend and him converge and take the flag without difficulty and the way she acts as if they have injured her gives him great satisfaction.

Another night around the fire, and conversation rendered them strangers. A good night's sleep and hearty breakfast and another game of capture the flag is pending. Today she is surprised to see him on the same team as her. She is not chosen as the flag defender and wonders if that's because she lost it yesterday but if everyone on her team was captured can they really hold her responsible. She is running and running until she can feel her cheeks flush and she is working so hard at not letting the footsteps she can hear behind her catch up to her she doesn't see the rock in front of her and trips and stumbles down the wooded path she is traveling. She continues to slide until she is falling, the only thing that goes through her mind is I'm dying and I never said thank you to him for helping with my backpack. She just stares for a second not being able to attach it to an owner until she hears:

"Uffffttt."

She follows the voice and sees the blonde hair, bronzed, pack carrying hero. She wonders why he just grunts instead of offering her a hand to get up. She looks at him and he is peculiarly flushed, for a minute she just attributes this to the exertion of the game but she is drawn to the fact that one of his shoes is off and there is a red spot on his ankle. She wonders if he broke something and her eyes focus and can see the wound better she gasps:

"You were bit by a snake? Let me go get help."

His arm points up and she turns around to follow where he points.

"Oh"

"It's ok; I already put my snake bite kit to it."

"Good thing you had that with you. We should still get you to a doctor, there has to be some way. Surely they will notice us gone very soon."

"I'm sure" He continues, but seems to be focusing on the pain and not on her words.

"Think I can climb up?" She says. Not sure if she's talking to anyone at all.

"I tried; I fell that's when I got bit."

"Oh Well, at least let me put the kit to the wound again, make me feel better."

It's then that notices the swollen knee. He doesn't even mention it. She takes the tool from his hand and applies it to his ankle where she can see the suction marks from him previously doing this, but it makes her feel useful.

"I didn't get to thank you for taking my pack yesterday, sure made a difference so thank you. My name is Symone."

"It was nothing, now you have attended my wound we're even. I am Ian."

"It's not a score, but if it were, we wouldn't be even until you get this looked at by a doctor."

"Oh no don't worry I don't even think it was a rattle snake."

"Oh yeah, then why bother with the snake bite kit."

She shakes her head at him and gets up to call for help and a hand comes to her arm.

"Might as well save your breath until we have heard they have captured the flag."

She knew there was always a lot of commotion when a flag was captured, but surely there was nothing to be heard at this distance yet she did not move.

"So, you don't like volleyball?"

"I would say I like it but I am very bad at it. I don't want to bring down the team, so I don't play."

"You sure hold your own at capture the flag."

"You patronizing me, I swear I would have given you a run for your money if Joe and you had not ganged up on me"

"Ha-ha, yeah lucky coincidence that."

They continue in a comfortable conversation. He talked about his adoptive family and she about her sister, stepsister although she was sure he had already noticed them. If other girls were around she always felt invisible and history, at least in her mind, had done nothing to prove her wrong.

Conversation veered from the normal get to know you questions to the more direct,

"So, do you always do the chivalrous thing and help damsels in distress out?" she asked.

"No," he laughed "I didn't think you were in distress just wanted to help out."

From a distance they heard the familiar shout of victory and those chasing the one with the flag. After a moment the shouts died and she said,

"I think it is safe to call for help now."

He doesn't even acknowledge because the conversation was keeping his mind off the pain of his knee and now it's throbbing again.

"Surely someone must hear me."

He just nods. After a few attempts she sits back down

"Ok, well at least there are two of us and I can make sure red streaks don't start running up your leg and you die. It would seem I have nothing better to do."

"Are you always this cavalier about the health of those who help you out?" His laughter gave away he was more tickled than anything.

"No I said thank you, I'm not cavalier but you're acting all brave and so I didn't think it would do to for me to act overly concerned."

"You're sweet. Really though I am ok."

"Besides, for all I know being stuck here might be helping. At least by being still I have heard you don't want to get the blood pumping and have the toxin travel."

"See there you go, nothing to worry about."

"Speak for yourself. The last time I was here a guy was helicoptered out. Ok so it was because his kid was in a car accident back home not because of anything here, I still have a healthy respect for hazards of the outdoors. Look at the situation we're in." But she said it very light heartedly.

They both laughed at this and conversation began about the worse accidents they had ever heard of. Of course she couldn't compete, but she suspected he embellished some of his stories. She did have to admit he didn't seem to be in pain and soon she forgot about his snake bit and just lost in the conversation. Apparently the same happened to him because next time he looks around its dark.

"Wow. I can't believe how long we have been sitting here talking. I guess no one heard you earlier."

"Neither can I, I will try again."

All of a sudden they hear someone call.

"Who's down there?"

"Symone and Ian, we both fell. One of us is injured."

"Hey I don't want to worry anyone." Ian interrupts

"I know but you are injured."

The person came back with reinforcements and rope but the ledge they were on was off to the side and harder to see in the dark so after a couple attempts that didn't it was decided that they would wait until morning when it was light.

'God I wish I had my coat," she says.

'Mine is around here somewhere."

All of a sudden she sees it askew off to his other side. She picks it up and puts it over him gently. Even in the dark she can see his eyes open and he says

'What about you?"

'I'll be fine."

"You're the one who mentioned a coat and besides how are you supposed to help me if you freeze, remember something about toxin, red streaks and me dying."

She giggles slightly, the sound makes him smile.

"Come on we can share it."

He lifts himself up to a more sitting position and holds out part of his coat to her. She slides beside him, instantly noticing the warmth of his body.

"Better?"

"Yes thanks"

"Now tell me a story." He says

"I would, but I think you're the one who is the story teller?"

"Hmm, I would ask you what that's supposed to mean, but by the sly smile you have on your face, I think I know."

"I don't know what you mean"

"Pfft, right."

He then begins one of this tales about another hiking excursion, fortunately the only eventfulness to that trip was they had forgotten some of their food and we're nearly starving by the time they returned.

"Best meal of my life when we hit the Denny's on our way home."

"That is a sad state of affairs if Denny's is your best meal."

"Indeed."

"Tell me another story, will you?"

So he told her about a trip to the beach with his family and his silly little brother going out too far and getting caught in an under toe and having to save him. Not much scared him but he felt goose bumps pop up at the fear he experienced that day. He also got surprised to hear a catch in his throat at describing how his little brother looked when he got him ashore. He looked at her through the corner of his eye and what he saw made him turn his head. She had fallen asleep on his shoulder.   The goose bumps and fear from his memories replaced by a strange twinge in his belly at the way her nose twitched in her sleep. How had he not felt her head on his shoulder? He was aware now. The way her soft hair tickled his neck as it touched. How her soft breathing turning white as soon as it hit the cold air. He tucked the coat over her shoulder and sunk down and closed his eyes even though he knew sleep would never come.

However when the next morning came it did find him asleep. So did Symone as she was the first to open her eyes. After she realized where she was she said:

"You think anyone back at camp is awake yet?"

He shrugged. "Anxious to get off this cliff and away from me are you?"

"I would think you were anxious to get up and see how we can get you medical help if needed."

"Maybe I would be but I don't think it's needed."

Their conversation was cut short from shouts from above. Indeed their friends from camp were up yet and after much disputing who would go first, Symone found herself being lifted and up the cliff before she knew it. The process of getting Ian out obviously more complicated due to his injuries, when he got to the top she found herself visually inspecting the swelling in his knee and the snake bite and decided she didn't agree with him it might need medical help but now their friends would help and everything would be ok. The daily routine of meals, campfires and piddling around the camp proceeded and nighttime came and found Symone reading next to the fire and all of a sudden a body unceremoniously plopped down next to her. Her attention sufficiently diverted from her book she said:

"Should you be resting?"

"I'm hardly running a marathon."

"No but didn't we talk about keeping still so toxins from your bite don't go to your heart."

"Yes, we also talked about being uncertain it was even a rattle snake. But if you get me my sleeping bag, I promise to stay put."

"Be right back."

She dashed off and was back before he knew it. After ensuring him comfortable enough that he could keep his promise to stay put she turned back to her book.

"Well, you could at least read to me."

She just laughed, again causing a strange sensation in his stomach, but he ignored and listened to her read. Her voice had a melody to it that relaxed him and he found himself closing his eyes. All of a sudden they opened, he realized she had stopped reading and was scooting away.

"Why did you stop?" he asked.

She spun around "Oh, you started me. I'm cold and tired and was going to go climb in my tent and in my own sleeping bag if you must know."

"Bring your sleeping bag next to the fire and keep reading. I was nearly asleep."

"Demanding and insulting, what would induce me to do what you ask?"

"Please? Besides no insult I was not falling asleep for boredom" he smiled a crooked smile that she knew must have melted a few hearts before. But she wouldn't give him the satisfaction.

"Does that ever work on anyone?" she scoffed

"Actually you'd be surprised," he continued "Come on, you feel bad for the poor patient don't you?"

"I shouldn't your shameless," but she was heading for her sleeping bag as she spoke.

She read for a while in her book about a mysterious stranger who came to town and strange murders began happening. A book like this would normally give her the creeps but she knew from the description that the stranger is not the bad guy but actually helps catch the killer. She paused and looked over and found him asleep. Further confirmation of this came when he didn't stir and instruct her to keep reading again. She watched the fire dance across his face and noticed sweat beading on his forehead. She gently touched nervous it meant fever but let out a breath she didn't know shed been holding when she felt the cool brow. She did feel the warmth radiating from his whole body and it reminded her of the night before on the cliff how it had offered not only warmth but comfort. Surely she would have been quite panicked had she been alone but she realized she had not been. She looked at his face again, such the mixture of a boy yet it had the rugged muscle of a mature man. How contradictory and intriguing, she just knew she could watch him sleep for hours. She remembered falling asleep on his shoulder and how he had smelled of pine trees. She shook her head and called herself stupid and cuddled down into her sleeping bag and let the fire lull her to sleep.

She woke up the next morning to the sound of her phone.

Where are you?

Why was her sister texting when they were in the tent together then she looked around and remembered she'd slept outside.

By the fire she texted back

She then saw her sister emerge from the tent and walk over to the coffee pot and gave her a sister a look that could only be saying. "Join me"

She groaned, loathed to leave the warmth of the sleeping bag. Shed swear she felt the warmth of the fire seeping somehow into her bag.

"What are you doing out here? Is something going on between you too?"

"Of course not" He just asked to be read to since he is trying to rest, and I fell asleep."

"Yeah, but that was only after retrieving your sleeping bag. It sounds premeditated to me."

"Hardly. Besides…"

Her voice cut off as her gaze drifted to the subject of her sister's interrogation. Her heart sunk as she saw his attention was now on Katherine. Katherine was her step-sister; her perfect, perky, beautiful younger step-sister. She loved her without question. So she didn't understand why it stung that they were talking except that it did.

"Besides he's more Katherine's type."

"She didn't sleep next to the fire with him?"

"I told you I didn't plan it I just fell asleep. Besides I need coffee if this conversation is going to last any longer."

The mention of coffee quite efficiently put an end to her sister's questioning. If anyone loved coffee more than Symone it was her sister Raven. After coffee it was breakfast duty, dish duty, cards. Plenty to keep her mind off Kathy and Ian, who seemed quite cozy chatting all morning and paired up at the card game. No, she didn't notice, not Symone. Ouch, why was she grinding her teeth?

Meanwhile, on the other side of camp . . .

Brian sauntered up to Ian and said,

"So, sleeping by the fire with one, and flirting up another. I should take notes."

"I don't know what you're talking about fool," was Ian's droll response.

"Oh I think you do. Just keep it cool ok?"

"Yes Sir." Ian quipped

"I'm serious. Katherine is cool, she can hold her own. But Symone is different, she's special. Crap! That makes it sound bad for Katherine, look I love them both but I know you, don't mess around with Symone. Don't ask me why I feel more protective. She is just . . . she's gentle, fragile even."

"While I don't think Symone would appreciate your assessment of her nor do I agree with it I assure you I have no intention of 'messing' with Symone."

"Good" Brian replied gruffly.

He stormed off and Ian was left counting to ten and taking deep breaths to calm himself down. He didn't know what bothered him more, the insinuation that he would hurt someone or that calling Symone 'fragile' didn't seem to do her justice. Yes, she was everything feminine and petite and delicate but there was more to her than that, an inner strength that should never be underestimated. What's more he felt that a lot of people did underestimate her and he didn't like that. He imagined she didn't like it either.

The rest of the day passed very uneventfully. Most everyone else played capture the flag again, but since Ian was still nursing a gimp knee he opted out and was resting by the fire. Symone watched him as she raced along the forest and became irritated when Kate joined him and was reading to him. She didn't know how but she felt as if she knew he was appearing to be asleep so she would stop instead of enjoying being read to as he had last night. She didn't know how she knew this but she did. And it might be wicked of her but it made her smile inside.

Conversation over dinner consisted of agreeing on how early they would pack out the next morning and how they would distribute the weight of Ian's pack so he wouldn't have to carry it. He didn't like anyone having to help him, and the conversation was making him very uncomfortable. He looked away and caught Symone's eye and was struck by a vivid awareness. She knew he hated this but what could they do. He cursed under his breath. He knew his knee wouldn't support the weight but he didn't care. He hated this; his mood had been so good the last few days, even when stranded on that god forsaken cliff. Why was he so irritated now? All off a sudden the crowd dispersed, to get desert, and snacks. Camping made one hungry after all.

"Don't feel bad, you helped me up, let us help you down?"

He heard sweetness in her voice, but it sounded too much like pity "I don't care, I don't like it."

"You're just being stubborn."

"I'm not helpless ok" he shot back before he could think. She had just equated her help up with his help down but he had not meant to imply she was helpless. Yet that was how it was going to come across, and how she would take it.

"Neither am I. I was not injured like you. I was just trying to help you don't have to be a jerk about it"

And he did feel like a jerk. He'd just got done being mad at someone underestimating her and he goes and makes her feel small himself. He wanted to go after her to apologize but she disappeared down the trail and instead of inviting gossip he would just sit and worry until she returned.

Chapter 2 – The Long Downhill Hike

He didn't talk to her before they set out but he knew the instant she returned. He felt her return. Crap, when did that start happening. Somewhere between berating himself to sleep for being a jerk and breakfast he packed and took the small amount of provisions his friends would allow him to carry and set out a good 15 minutes ahead of everyone because he didn't want to slow them down so he gave himself a head start to guarantee that he wouldn't.

He walked and walked until his knee was throbbing and took a seat by a rock by the creek. He had always enjoyed nature, and not as a hunter or fisherman but as an observer. The sounds and smells and sights. There was a bird in the tree singing as if it was announcing spring and praising the rushing water. There was the lush grass that lined the trail and the magnificently fragrant pine trees.

He wrote about it sometimes, which made him feel at peace, a peace he rarely had. In fact, the peace he found in nature and with his writing was what he thought kept him sane. He knew he had baggage and issues but when he was in nature or writing about it he thought he disguised it pretty well. Apparently, not well enough not to lash out people for no reason though. He was back to feeling like a jerk. Well if he were honest, he had not stopped feeling guilty about yelling at her, she'd just been trying help after all.

Finally the sound of voices penetrated his thoughts and he realized the rest of his group just passed him. Crap! There goes the head start.

Immediately, he gets up and starts after them. It would prove that he needed help if he was last down the mountain after all. He plugs a long at a faster pace than before, but still nothing compared to his pace up the mountain. He was sweating because of the pain in his knee yet he plugged on. He kept going until even his snake bite which had gotten much better started irritating him. He was struggling but still hobbling along wondering why he had not caught his friends when all of a sudden he turns a corner and perched on a rock while scooping water into her canteen is Symone. He immediately feels better and is shocked at his response but chocks it up to being glad to have an opportunity to apologize. She just set there after she finished her drink and was serenely gazing at nature in an all too familiar way for him. When it became obvious she was not going to notice his presence he spoke:

"I love staring at nature too."

"Hey, I thought you were ahead of us."

"I was but I got caught day dreaming and got lapped.

"I see, well since I know appearing helpless but being the last one down would kill you don't let me keep you."

"I deserve that, I wanted to apologize. I am not a very good patient."

"I learned that being stuck on that cliff with you, but apology accepted," was her rejoinder.

"Well, they will think something happened to us if we don't stop daydreaming."

She took that as a cue and stood up, wincing slightly at the twisted ankle that had made her stop. He noticed it.

"I'm not the only gimpy one I see."

"I only twisted my ankle slightly, nothing compared to your knee, but yeah it let me know it's there."

"When did you do that?"

"Last night, I took a walk in the dark and didn't see this hole. It's ok really."

He winced inwardly realizing that her walk was after his outburst. He cleared his throat and said:

"Shall we?"

She responded by advancing on the trail ahead of him. After sometime of following her he began day dreaming and his thoughts drifted to the view ahead of him and he realized if he were any other guy he would be enjoying the view of her backside. But the idea of another guy watching her was distasteful. What was happening, he needed to get a hold of himself. He knew relationships were out of the question for him and Symone was not the kind of girl you dallied with, she was relationship material for sure. He tried to put his mind on other things, nature he focused on nature. This immediately made him feel better and for a long time they walked along in a comfortable silence. A silent agreement to stop came to them after a while and he took the opportunity to fill his canteen.

"Want me to fill yours too?"

"No, it's still pretty full."

Silence and then:

"This is going to sound very random but when we get back you should totally ask my sister Kate out, you two seemed to click and I think she likes you."

He nearly spit out his water:

"You barely know me but you want me to ask out your sister?"

"A night on the cliff and by the fire was enough to tell me you're a nice guy, so yeah. I know you think she's pretty, everyone thinks she's pretty."

He winced at her obvious awareness of the attention her sister got.

"Hey, I hope I didn't give anyone the wrong idea because she is nice and all but I don't think she's my type. Furthermore I'm most certainly not her type. I'm not anyone's type."

"Oh" was all she said.

Inwardly, she didn't know which emotion was bigger. Giddiness that he didn't want to go out with her or curiosity about why he thought he was not anyone's type. Curiosity was very strong but he said it so matter of fact she didn't think it appropriate to ask any questions. But then he offered:

"Sorry to be so blunt he continued, I'm just not ready or interested in romantic relationships."

She had expected more explanation but none was forthcoming and she was left feeling that the curiosity would get the better of her if she didn't find a change of subject, and soon.

"So, you like nature a lot huh?"

"Yes, I do. I love the outdoors, it's so peaceful."

"I agree" she responded, happy to be past the awkward exchange about relationships.

They began swapping stories about reasons for their love of nature and eased and it became obvious they had this in common. It obviously made him feel comfortable because before he knew it he was telling her about his writing.

"I would love to read them some time." He heard her say

No one else knew about his writing let alone had ever read them. Yet he felt himself almost eager to let her read them

"Yeah that would be cool, when we get back."

She smiled. They probably would have kept talking but the sky opened up and it started raining and they silently agreed that they had better proceed before it got worse. It was slow going due to their injuries, she was trying to be stoic but her sprain really did hurt. The wet was a reprieve from the heat at first but then it just soaked through to the skin. It got heavier until it just made your shorts chafe between your legs and made you all around miserable. Conversation was few and far between but every once in a while one would catch the others eye and a meaningful exchange would occur completely without words. Symone began to wonder what it meant, she had never felt such an instant connection with someone before and while she liked it, it scared her at the same time. It scared her a lot.

Many minutes later they decided if they didn't get moving down the trail the search and rescue team would be sent for them and neither of them wanted that. Unlike before conversation did happen, they discussed their families, he'd met Symone's sisters so he talked about his brother and sister and parents. All of a sudden he asked:

"Did you and Brian ever date?"

A laugh escaped before she could answer "No I'm pretty sure he thinks of me more as a sister than anything else."

"Most guys do." (She muttered under her breath but he caught it anyway)

"Why do you ask?"

It made sense that Brian would be protective of someone he felt like a sister about but he was much more interested in why she felt most guys felt that way.

"No reason. Why do you think guys feel for you as a sister?"

"I don't know, I'm everyone's friend just not the stuff of relationships I guess." she deflected

He remembered thinking she was exactly the stuff relationships were made of but of course he didn't repeat it. He didn't want to even think it considering he definitely didn't want a relationship.

"Sometimes the best relationships start as friendships." He said just making conversation

"Ugh, that is a platitude my mother would use. Are you trying to set up Brian or me?"

"Neither. Please forget I said anything it was silly." Tickled at the comparison to her mother, he was quite sure he had never said anything that compared to a mother before and quite unsettled about the irksome feeling that came at the thought of setting her up with anyone.

"I have a proposal." She said distracting him from his reverie. "I won't try to set you up with my sister Kate and you won't try to set me up with Brian."

"Deal," he easily agreed. His lopsided grin crossing his face in a manner she could only read as relief.

"I'm just impressed we can keep walking and talk at the same time. We seemed to be only able to do one at a time earlier."

"Hey I am capable of conversation while I walk, you're the quiet one?" he quipped.

"I admit I am not the perfect conversationalist, one of my many faults you'll find."

"I will huh, that infers we will be encountering each other after this trip," he said wickedly hoping it would set her off balance.

"Oh I would never infer that. We do have friends in common obviously it's not out the realm of possibility that we would run into each other and that is all I was saying," she replied.

He was impressed with her ready reply. And yet it confused him. He had seen her shy and at a loss for words with much less provocation this weekend. He definitely had been trying to provoke her this time and she rose to the challenge splendidly. What a splendid contradiction. He wouldn't try to dissect why he had noticed her interactions with others so much or what that meant. He most definitely wanted to encounter her again after this trip. After all, it didn't have to lead to a relationship did it?

"You're right of course. Brian is one of my best friends. We hang out a lot. We probably will run into each other."

Her only response was a smile and to keep on walking. She inwardly smacked herself on the forehead and a reality check. Of course he was not concerned about connecting up again, why would he. She wouldn't give him the satisfaction of knowing that that smarted. She just needed to remember this was her, she was forgettable.

However, she began to slow down and her face got somber. He caught sight of it while she turned a particularly extreme switchback and he wondered what had happened to change her mood. Weren't they joking around just minutes ago?

"Is everything ok? Do you need another break?"

"Nope I'm great. Well I'm tired but we'll never get down if we don't keep going, right?"

"I guess so, but it is not a race either."

"I guess not," she replied. She wanted to continue by saying 'the sooner we're down the sooner we're out of each other's company. She knew she was being irrational but she couldn't shake the feeling he would rather be with someone like Kate, everyone always preferred her. She was told she wore her feelings on her sleeve, she guessed she was right. After all he had asked her if something was wrong, it was probably all over her face.

"Before we go our separate ways today, don't let me leave without getting your number today ok," his voice disturbing her irrational thoughts so completely she almost startled.

"Ok. I don't guarantee I will remember but I will try."

The smile she flashed made him nearly stop in his tracks. Not because of a dazzling smile but her eyes. They weren't something you noticed right away but there was a spark. They were also so honest you could see yourself in them. He prided himself on being good at telling people what they would want to hear but he couldn't imagine fibbing even a little bit to her, or to be precise to those eyes.

Another round of comfortable conversation ensued. It didn't seem they had much in common, she was super girly with a love for musicals and he was into extreme sports with a love for anything well, extreme. However there was comfort even in acknowledging those differences. The differences seemed to fit the perception of each were each developing of the other. All of a sudden he pipes off with:

"Ok, your first sexual experience?"

"Excuse me? Inappropriate much?"

"Only in a good way. Come on don't be a prude."

"Well, prude is going to take on a whole new meaning when I say not yet."

"Your only a prude if not yet means you're not going to tell me yet. The other I respect."

"Thanks, most people find it weird, or don't understand is probably a more fair statement."
"It is rare so you're probably right." And he just continues walking

"Well?" She calls out from behind him

"Well, what? I can't divulge that kind of information without some kind of reciprocation."

"If telling you not yet is not reciprocating, I don't know what is. Besides you brought it up so spill."

"Got me there 'breezy'"

He begins on a tale of a trip to summer camp in his teens where a girl climbed into his tent and threw herself at him. She was a counselor so she got fired when it was discovered she got pregnant from one of the kids. He said he didn't hear from her until she popped on her doorstep to tell him he was a father and that they were friends when it came to their child but that was the extent of it. He sounded very proud of his son. He said he couldn't wait until he was old enough to bring on a trip like this and that his name was Liam. She couldn't help but smile over how he gushed over his son.

"Two questions, how old is your son? And breezy?"

"He is three and yes breezy, when we were on the cliff I noticed you smelled like the ocean, what kind of body wash do you use?"

"It is unscented; I don't like chemicals so it is organic. I have a hard time believing that on a sweaty camping weekend you smelled me body wash."

"Well I did. Someone smelling that clean after a weekend roughing it like this is not something you make up"

They walked on in silence for a while after that. His comment about her smelling clean like the ocean brought to mind she thought he smelled like the pine trees. Someone might think that weird considering they were surrounded by them so he had dismissed it. After all they were stranded on a cliff; their minds were most likely just playing tricks on them. This time it was her turn to break the silence:

"So, you get to see your son on a regular basis?"

"Yeah every other weekend deal. I hate it, but she is a good mother so I can't complain too much."

"So I don't know your middle name but I know about your first experience and the fact that you have a three year old son. That's a new one for me."

He rolls his head back and laughs. "For me also. Tell me, does everyone spill their life story when they first meet you?"

"You hardly told me your life story, but no. Come to think of it, I have never spent a night stuck on a cliff with someone before, so it is sure a weekend for firsts."

"It sure is. Oh and I will finish my life story next time we meet, wouldn't want to overwhelm you."

It was her turn to laugh heartily. "I appreciate you holding back"

"I can't help but feeling gipped though, I know you reciprocated but my story led to you knowing two things about me. Somehow it doesn't seem fair."

"What do you want to know?"

"Something I wouldn't expect, something that would surprise people to find out about you."

"I love thrills, the dive devil at magic mountain, parasailing, zip lines things like that."

"That doesn't surprise me, it might most folks. They don't look at you closely enough. I can definitely see that about you. You're reserved for sure, but there are such depths to your eyes. Well, let's just say people do you and themselves a disservice if they don't look twice."

"I'm going to choose to take that as a compliment."

"You should."

"What is it by the way?"

"What is what?"

"Your middle name, of course. Did we not already establish that that is part of the criteria for getting to know someone?"

"It is Xavier, and I don't know about criteria, it just sounded random."

"Random it may have been, but it serves as notice that I don't let subject matters drop. I have far too good of a memory for that."

"Good memory got it. That can be a blessing and a curse."

"Definitely, when it is a curse it's a bad one."

"It sounds like there is story there."

However, before she could respond or he could inquire further, they found themselves rounding the clearing into the trail end and their friends descended upon them en mass.

Some sincere inquiries about their injuries and some lighthearted ribbing about the amount of time spent together, and how long it took to descend the mountain ensued. Ian caught Symone's eyes with this and gave her half a smile. She returned it with a shy one of her own.

The general consensus was they deserved a bbq or picnic before returning home so people dove into their packs and an eclectic assortment meal was well on its way. Ian and Symone both lost interest fast and unbeknownst to each other sought out their friends and said their good byes and headed to their cars.

Symone opened her door when she heard an already increasingly familiar voice.

"Breezy"

"I sincerely hope you don't expect me to answer to that moniker."

He flashed his devastating smile and said;

"Sure I do. Just kidding. I just wanted to get your number"

She rattles off her phone number and asks him to text her so she will in turn have his. They say good bye, get in their respective cars and drive home.

Symone drops her things right inside the door and leaves a trail of clothes all the way to the shower. She loses all sense of time relaxing in the shower as she allows it to wash all the dirt and pain from her injuries away. She exits the shower and dons a robe and is kicking back on the couch when her pack buzzes. She leans over and retrieves her phone to see the following message:

Here's my number. Don't forget that you owe me a life story.

She smiles as she types back:

I won't forget. I do hate being in debt. LOL BTW Stay off Cliffs!

Before she gets a reply she succumbs to the fatigue of the trip and the comfort of her overstuffed cushions and falls asleep. She dreams of blue skies and a man that smells like pine.

She is awoken by the sound of her phone buzzing and picks it up:

"Hello?"

"Symone, its Kat. Up for breakfast?"

"Depends, how soon do I have to be ready and does it include coffee."

"Half an hour and you bet."

"Ok, can you pick me up?"

"Sure, k bye"

"Bye"

Symone wanders to the bedroom and puts on a pink tank top and jean shorts and sandals. She pulls her hair in ponytail to try to tame the unruly curls and calls it good. She is not trying to impress Kat anyway. They had not done breakfast lately and she would be surprised Kat was so perky already but that was her, bright as sunshine even after that trip.

She felt a small reminder of her injury when she leaned on the leg with the sprained ankle but was happy to say it was not nearly as bad as it had been. She just got done brushing her teeth when the doorbell rings.

"Did someone order a grande vanilla latte?"

"Have I told you lately that I love you?"

"No but that goes without saying."

Symone shuts the door behind her and allows Kat to lead her to the car.

"Couldn't get Raven up?" Symone asks Kat. It is a widely known family secret that Raven enjoys her sleep as much as she does her coffee. No breakfast could tempt her to join them.

"Of course not."

Symone sips her coffee as she listens to Kat talk about the picnic and Brian, both her interest in and attention from him, and how much she and Ian were missed.

"If I didn't know better, I would think you two left together."

"Well, glad to hear you know better. We may have left at the same time but we didn't leave together."

They pulled into the restaurant and Symone sighed at her sister's choice of restaurant. It was one of those healthy, vegan places Kat loved. She possessively tugged her coffee cup to her and then took another sip. When Kat opened the door to the restaurant Symone stopped in her tracks. What she thought was a quiet sisterly breakfast was obviously a continuation of yesterday's picnic. The whole camping group was there. It wasn't that Symone was unhappy to see them but she knew how she looked, how little time she took to get ready this morning.

"Kat, I thought it was just going to be us."

"No, I know this is not your favorite. Brian suggested it, because he heard me say I liked it probably. You have your coffee, you're fine right?"

"Yeah sure."

Spots across from Brian and Ian were the only seats. Kat sat down across from Brian leaving Symone across from Ian. He was talking to the guy on his right but lifted his eyes and when his eyes landed on her coffee he smiled.

She sat and sipped and offered responses when addressed but otherwise was happy to simply observe the conversation. When the guy on Ian's right turned his attention in turn to his right, Ian immediately directed his attention to Symone:

"You survived?"

"Yes, thanks to a hot shower, and this coffee."

"Shower did feel great. Can't say the same for coffee, never liked it.

"For not having had coffee, you look bright eyed and bushy tailed. You're not one of those annoying morning people are you?"

"Depends on what you find annoying. I like to take an early morning jog before work. Does that count?"

"No, as long as you're not overly cheerful. You in-shape people do make us normal folks look bad though."

"Ah, but how I can help people with their packs if I don't stay in shape."

"True, and since I know how appreciative I was I wouldn't want the next normal person to not be helped. Therefore keep up the jogging."

That elicited a chuckle. "Only because you approve."

"I do."

She sipped her coffee and the group conversation took over as the topic of meeting for a movie Friday night came up. He gave her a look that could only be asking if she was going to which she shook her head. At the same time she heard;

"Of course Symone and I are going."

Ian couldn't decide what was funnier, the look on Symone's face or when she choked on her surprise at Kats comment.

"I guess I am," she softly whispered across the table. To which he only smiled in response.

On the ride home Symone asked Kat why she spoke for her about going to the movies this weekend. To which Kat ribbed her about being a homebody and not having any plans.

"Besides, if Brian goes he will drag Ian and you know that you want to see him again."

Symone didn't respond to this. She was equally loathed to admit that her sister was right as she was to admit that she did want to see Ian again as she was surprised her sister picked up on her interest in him. Kat was notoriously oblivious to anything in which she was not involved.

After being dropped off Symone dug into her chores. She would love to say she was a neat freak but such was not the case. She knew that if she didn't address the laundry from the trip now, come time for work on Monday her pack would still be sitting by her door. She didn't want to have to admit that to anyone.

On the other side of town

Ian was on the phone with his son's mom making arrangements to see him next

"I thought you said you were fine with swapping weekends. Now because you have plans I can't see him?"

"I'm sorry. It just came up while you were camping and had no service. My mom's keeping him."

"How about I keep him for you? It can count as my weekend since I was gone last weekend."

"My mom will be disappointed to not spend time with him but sure. I will let her know about the change in plans."

"Ok, when do you want me to pick him up?"

They finished the plans for the following weekend and hung up. He shrugged off the irritation that always accompanied talking to her. He decided to take a run. Later that day, between the endorphins from the running and hot shower he was smiling. She's right; a hot shower makes everything better. Again he was surprised by how easily she came to mind.

Symone poured herself a cup of coffee and sat down on the couch. Thank god she had taken this whole week off. Camping aside, she needed the rest. She had been working crazy, long hours. Instead of reading in bed at night she had found herself falling asleep the minute her head hit the pillow.   She would enjoy the day of peace and quiet. Then the door opened:

"Hey sis I hope you made coffee."

"Of course" she sighed

Raven grabbed herself a cup and plopped own beside her on the couch.

"So, Kat is into Brian"

"Yes"

"I think he is in to her too"

"Aren't most guys?"

"I know. Her interest is what surprises me. You know how she is. She doesn't usually think about the guy when she's not around him. You know?"

"Uhhhhmmm"

"Are one word syllables all I'm going to get out of you today?"

There wasn't anyone else who could and would talk to her like her sister Raven. But since it was Raven she just arched her eye brow and replied:

"Maybe"

"What is up with you and Ian anyway?"

"Nothing, absolutely nothing," because that is what Symone believed.

Chapter 3 – A Meeting of the Minds

When Raven and Kat picked up Symone she was awestruck by the difference in her two sisters.   I know they weren't related by blood but you would think being raised together would have brought out some similarities. It wasn't just appearance either. Don't get me wrong, they looked different two. Kat was tall and striking with her olive complexion and dark ebony hair. Raven was petite like Symone but almost ethereal in her blonde hair and pixie haircut. The major differences were there personalities though. Kat was used to being noticed instead taking notice of anything or anyone else. On the other hand, Raven noticed everything, sometimes she knew things about Symone before Symone knew them about herself. Kat and Raven both had big personalities, but while Kat was always the center of attention Raven stood out because you knew she didn't care what people thought. Not to say that Kat was shallow or Raven was aggressive in her independence. They were both the most sensitive, generous people she had ever met. She couldn't love anyone more. She just couldn't imagine two polar opposites. Where did that leave Symone? She was exactly in the middle. She was not tall and striking like Kat or blonde and ethereal like Raven. She didn't have Kat's magnetism or Raven's strength and independence. She was just Symone, the middle child. This is why she was trying not to think about Ian, and making a sad attempt at dismissing her attraction to him. Why would someone like him ever take an interest in her? She was convinced they wouldn't.

Symone would have been surprised just how many times she had come into Ian's mind this week. He was surprised too but only because usually women he meant disappeared from his mind as fast as the pain in his sprained ankle had. People just hadn't usually stayed in his life long enough to make an impression, other than his mother, brother, and son of course. She thought of how at ease he had felt around her, the easy going manner which she accommodated his moodiness or demands to read to him. He felt a little disappointment that they would all be watching a movie tonight leaving little time for conversation.

The group assembles in front of theater and the general consensus is a horror movie. Symone crinkles her nose at the mention of the movie.

"You don't want to watch it?"

She was startled that anyone had seen her reaction. She turned to Ian and shyly said;

"Not really"

"Then what shall we watch?"

"Oh I don't know let's see." She joins him in reading the marquee.

"How about watching the silly comedy?"

'Honestly, that looks like something I'd rent or watch on television but not pay to see in the theater."

"How about a romantic comedy?"

"Definite television material. I know how about that mystery/adventure movie?"

"Ok, that is definitely theater worthy."

He turns his attention to the group and advises them that they are seeing something different and the group immediately starts communicating their regrets. Raven arches an eyebrow at Symone and gives her a knowing glance to which Symone only response is to roll her eyes. Symone now notices that the movie the group is seeing begins and ends a full hour before theirs. The group now heads in leaving just the two of them. There is a slightly awkward silence until:

"I hope I just didn't keep you from seeing a movie you wanted to see," says Symone.

"Not at all, anything that is going to make me look silly for getting scared is definitely television material. Have you had your caffeine for the day?"

"No actually I got sidetracked with a photo album project this morning so I forgot it."

"There is a great coffee shop around the corner, we got an hour. What do you say?"

"I say, you're my hero."

"I helped you up a mountain, not to mention spent the night on a cliff with you, but getting you coffee makes me your hero?"

"That just shows you how high coffee ranks with me."

"Oh is that it?"

Symone was still laughing when he held the door to the coffee shop open for her. Symone didn't know if was how comfortable she felt around him or the wonderful smells in the coffee shop, probably both, but she loved this place. They placed their orders and took their seats.

"So what do you do for a living?"

"I work for oil companies, environmental work, respond to spills that type of thing."

"Really did you work that one in the gulf?"

"Well I helped, that wasn't my company but we were consulted on it. How about you?"

"I work as a freelance magazine photographer. I did work for sports but I like more landscape, scenery."

"Paid to travel? That must be nice. Have I seen any of your work?"

"I don't know. Do you like National Geographic?"

"Nat Geo, I love it. I'm impressed."

"Enough about me though, I remember someone owing someone a life story."

He had shrugged off her compliment and re-directed attention at her. For such a remarkable guy she couldn't believe he was uncomfortable with praise and attention. It was endearing and intriguing.

"Ok, well when I was seven. Just Kidding. Not much to tell. My mom died when I was born. My dad said she was the love of his life but he couldn't stand to be alone so he was married three more times until he married Kat's mom. Three years later Raven was born. We've been one happy family ever since."

"Did you and Kat like each other at first?"

"No, I wanted all of my father's attention for myself. Her dad had died so she ate up his attention and it would drive me nuts. We shared a room though so we kind of were forced to be close. And of course we had to join forces when Raven was born. Not really. We both loved that baby, fought over who loved her more from the day they brought her home. That's the first thing we agreed on actually, loving her."

"Are you close to your step-mom?"

"Now I am. At first I kept my distance because I thought she'd either die like my mom or my dad would cheat on her like he did the others. But she didn't die and knows how to keep my dad in line, so… yeah."

"So I know about the first time thing, but serious relationships?"

One, he pursued me for nine months before I would go out with him. It was like after we did he stopped putting any effort into the relationship at all. I complained about that, he said I was pushing him away, who knows maybe he's right. How about you?"

Relationships? Nope. I mean I've dated. It's not because I'm afraid of commitment either. I know you're thinking it."

If not commitment issues, then what is it?" she asked with a smile

I don't know. I've never met anyone that makes me want to commit to them. My mother and brother are they only relationships in my life, well my friends like Brian and my son of course."

I understand that, I think seeing my father remarry made me hesitant to commit. Maybe that was my problem with Jeremy."

"Speaking of commitments and relationships . . ."

He got embarrassed by how that sounded, he turned red. So did Symone.

"By relationship, I meant my relationship with my son. I am going to take my son to the zoo next Saturday. Would you like to join us?"

"I understood what you meant. And Yes. If you're sure I wouldn't be imposing on guy time."

He smiled at her, and assured her that would not be the case. He advised her that since his son would spend the night with him on Friday so they could plan on picking her up early Saturday morning so they could be there when it opened. She agreed eagerly even though she cringed inside at getting up that early.

Unbeknownst to them not only had they missed their movie, the one their friends attended was over. They were only alerted to this by them all loudly joining them in the coffee shop. Brian slapped Ian on the back similarly to how Raven bumped Symone's hip. The mood was broken, as the coffee shop wasn't amenable to big groups. Everyone said goodbye and Symone found herself in the car with Raven and Kat. Raven started discussing the parts of the movie she enjoyed the most. For such a dainty, feminine looking thing, Raven could hang with the best of them when it came to horror movies.

"Ugh I didn't like it. I would have rather seen the romantic comedy," Kat said.

"You didn't mind squeezing Brian's arm when the scary parts happened. You can't do that in a romantic comedy," Raven countered.

"No, I didn't mind that. Just wait until you're interested in someone, you'll do the same thing."

Raven's only response was a snicker. Then she said:

"I got an idea, sister sleepover. It's been too long."

"Whose place," was Kats eager agreement

"Mine, sleepovers mean sharing, and I want my stuff." Symone requested.

"Fine" Kat and Raven said in unison.

To Symone's relief Kat's eagerness to discuss her burgeoning relationship with Brian kept Raven from grilling Symone about her and Ian. After several attempts and being rebuffed Raven finally gave in but gave Symone a look she knew to mean, 'This is not over." After all, Raven was the baby and maybe a little too used to getting her own way. They sipped wine and enjoyed the camaraderie and rivalry that can only be found with siblings. They danced, talked silly about boys, and when they could not keep their eyes open any longer, borrowed pajamas, and collapsed into Symone's king size bed.

Symone awoke to the most amazing smells coming from her kitchen the next morning.

"Good morning, what smells good?" She asked.

"Pinwheels and flavored coffee," Kat responded.

"OMG I don't know what I did to deserve you but remind me to do it again."

They sat down and enjoyed their pastries and coffee. Symone asked questions about Brian, hesitant to mention the plans she had with Ian next weekend. It's not that she didn't tell her sisters. She just wanted something that was only hers.

An hour later Raven awoke and grabbed a cup of coffee and joined them. All of a sudden her phone buzzes.

"Hey girls, dad is face-timing me." Symone said.

"Hey dad" They all greet him in unison.

"Well good, now I don't have to ask you if you know where your sisters are" he responded.

"Yeah we had a sleepover daddy," Raven adds.

"Then I'm surprised your awake already sleepyhead. By the way Kat, Symone your mother wants to make sure you got your tickets for your visit."

"We did" they assured him.

This was the best time of the week, Sunday. No running to work, no having to be anywhere. Being able to spend it visiting with loved ones just added to the joy.

On the other side of town

"So you'll pick me up Friday night daddy?" came a little voice over face-time.

"That's right buddy, right after work." Ian assured him.

"And we'll go see the lion?"

"Yes, a lion and many other animals. Do you like monkeys" Ian asked?

"Daddy, you know I like monkeys"

"I know you are a monkey." Ian said.

"Daddy," came a giggle. "Ok mom. Daddy I got to go eat breakfast. I love you"

"Ok bud, I love you too." Ian said and the line went dead.

Ian hadn't been able to go for his run because the call from his son came so early, so he changed and left for his run. After he returned and showered he sat down to work on his latest project. It was the mountain they had hiked and camped on. His thoughts naturally kept returning to the trip, the beauty, the smells; the campfire, and a singular smell of the sea that he always smells near her. He shrugged off his thoughts and tried to concentrate on his project again. The sooner he accomplished that this week the soon her could see his son Friday. He wouldn't focus on the fact that he had an extra special reason to enjoy this visit with his son. He wouldn't focus on that because he just didn't know what to do with those thoughts.

Symone arose that Monday morning and headed into work. She sat down at her desk and started reading her emails and was reviewing an emergency response plan for a plant in a very sensitive environmental area. She compiled a list of things the plan was missing and equipment she knew to be required by law. She was responding with her findings when Raven popped in.

"Care to grab lunch?"

"Lunch? What time is it?" Symone responded looking at her computer for the time. "11:30! WOW! It feels like I just got here, where did this morning go?"

"Exactly, you need to get out of the office for lunch. Let's go," was Raven's brusque rejoinder.

"Where are we going?" asked Symone.

"Let's eat anywhere but that vegan place around the corner. Kat loves that place i know but... "

"Agreed. Let's go."

They ordered lunch and were making small talk. Lunch came and Raven asked:

"So, I'm going shopping this weekend for new stuff for the trip to see mom and dad. Want to come with?"

"I can't. I have other plans." Symone responded.

"What other plans?" Raven sassily asked.

"Nosy much? Just plans."

"Why so secretive?" Raven responded. "BTW, I'm ignoring the nosy comment. It is not worth my mention."

"And yet you did. It is not a secret. Ian has his son and he asked me to go to the zoo with them."

"You're meeting his kid?" Raven asked, flabbergasted.

"No," Symone almost screamed, "It's not like that. I'm not meeting his kid like that. We just enjoy each other's company."

"Ok, I accept that. You were thrown together a lot while camping. But I want details when you get home." Raven said

"Yes, I promise. Can we talk about something else now?"

"Sure, can you believe our parent's live in South America?" Raven asked

"No I can't. Hurry up and eat, I got to get back to work," was Symone's only response.

The rest of the week went much the same, without the nice lunch break Symone's sister offered that Monday. Before she knew it, it was Friday and she was received the following text:

See ya in the morning

To which she responded:

Bright and early.

She awoke before her alarm the next morning. She selected a pair of beige capris and a pretty white blouse with sandals. She ran the brush through her hair and thought about makeup. She applied mascara and lip gloss and stopped. It was just the zoo after all. She put on her matching beige sandals and was thinking about coffee when the doorbell rang.

"Did someone order Starbucks?" Ian asked.

"Oh, you know the way to a woman's heart," Symone said as she took the coffee and shut the door behind her.

Taking in the boy "Don't you two look handsome?"

"Say thank you Jimmy."

"Thank you," came the cutest voice Symone had ever heard.

"Shall we?" Ian asked.

Ian put Jimmy in his seat and opened the door for Symone. The zoo wasn't that far away but Symone had never been.

"Funny I have lived here all my life but never been here." Symone offered.

"That makes three of us," Ian responded

"First time," came the little voice again.

"He is seriously adorable," Symone said.

"Thanks, I think so but, you know, I am biased." Ian gushed. As he said this, Jimmy lunged out of the car door at his father.

"Monkey, daddy. Let's go see the monkeys." Little Jimmy demanded.

"I'm sorry about that. He's just a little bit excited." Ian apologized.

"No apology necessary, I do believe someone asked for monkeys. Let's go." Symone encouraged.

Symone, Ian, and Jimmy saw turtles, bears, lions, and all manner of reptiles and birds. However, by far the favorite exhibit was the monkeys. A worker happened to be out and Jimmy got to hold a spider monkey. Symone took pictures of Ian and Jimmy. With the worker around, Ian insisted he take the camera and get one of her in it with them.

Lunch consisted of hot dogs, to Jimmy's delight. Of course, he was having so much fun he probably wouldn't have noticed if he didn't eat. While Ian was talking to Symone about the story that made Jimmy fall in love with monkey's Ian's cell phone rang.

"Hello"

"What do you mean? I thought you were out of town."

"Does it have to be tonight? We're having a great day at the zoo."

"Ok, see ya then."

Symone could tell it was Jimmy's mother, by the one end of the conversation. Then the phone rang again.

"Hello."

Really, that is good news."

Thank you for calling. Thank you so much."

He hung up the phone and the tense shoulders created by the first conversation had relaxed a little.

That news didn't make up for the first call but it sure helped." Ian explained. "Unfortunately Jimmy can't stay the whole weekend, his mom wants him home tonight."

Oh I'm sorry." Symone wondered about a mother trying to keep father and son apart. "And the good news is?"

The magazine wants to use my pictures from the mountain for the next issue. Front page. Cover. I've been wanting that forever."

Congratulations Ian."

Ok, shall we go see if there is anything in the gift shop we can't live without?" Ian asked Jimmy

Yes. Daddy, can Sim carry me?"

Sure if you ask nicely and don't demand."

Sim would you carry me, I'm not manding."

Of course I would" she replied. Really how could she deny him?

The day rounded off with pizza. The adults talked while Jimmy ran the obstacle course in the play area.

He is going to sleep so good tonight." Symone commented, watching Jimmy's antics.

Yeah I wish I didn't have to take him home."

I'm so sorry, do you get next weekend?"

No, she claims since I missed last weekend, I am forfeiting the time." Ian explained.

They had had a wonderful day. To say that the phone call had put a damper on spirits wouldn't be inn accurate though. Jimmy fell asleep on the way home. Symone kissed his forehead as she got out of the car. Ian walked her to the door.

"You didn't have to do that, I know you got to get him home."

"I just wanted to apologize for getting bummed out. I didn't mean for that to ruin your day."

"It most definitely didn't ruin my day. Jimmy is such a delight. Really the company was so enjoyable. Thanks for letting me tag along." Symone assured him.

"You're being generous. We'll have to do today over again sometime. A rain check, if you will" Ian explained.

"If you insist, I'm game." Symone said while laughing.

"Ok bye." Ian said as he reached in to hug her.

She returned the hug. As he turned and walked back to the car, she watched his broad shoulders tailor down into a slim waist and imagined those arms around her. She was thinking about how she was already in trouble.

He looked up right before he got in the car just in time to see her turn and walk in the house. Even the way her hair swished made him think of the ocean. He didn't know why, even though her legs couldn't be called long, he was imagining them wrapped around his waist.

She was pouring a glass of wine when her phone buzzed.

Jimmy said to tell Sim good night.

She typed

Tell Jimmy thank you for a wonderful day.

Another beep

Can you send me the pics from today? I didn't seem to take any with my phone.

She did. She thought of sending the one of the three of them but didn't want to be presumptuous that he would want that one.

Another beep

Where is the one the zookeeper took?

Symone quickly forwards the requested picture

Another beep

Thanks. I had a great time. Good night.

Symone is awakened the next morning by her phone ringing.

"Hello"

"Hey, so how did it go yesterday?" came Raven's voice, exceedingly cheery and bright.

"Raven, what are you doing up already?" asks Symone as she looks at the time. Raven is less of a morning person than she is.

"Well, I was too excited to sleep well. I wanted to hear about your day."

"It was fine. We were having fun until the boy's mom called and wanted him home. That kind of threw a damp blanket on the day."

"Aww, that sucks." Raven said. "So tell me. Is there chemistry between you and Ian?"

"Tell me why you sound so excited about my day at the zoo?"

Symone shouldn't have been surprised at Raven's excitement. Once she was awake and going, she was always going a mile a minute, like a bird. What an appropriate name she had.

"Tell me why you're not more excited. Have some coffee already. I don't know I want you to be happy, I want to live vicariously through you, since I haven't met anyone."

"Well I hate to burst your bubble, but we are just friends. I mean he is attractive and adorable with his son, but . . . you're right I need coffee. Can we talk about this later?"

"Yeah. Love You. Bye."

"Love you too Rav, Bye."

Symone drank her coffee and decided to use the beautiful day to take a walk in the park. She set out on the trail and was a good way into the walk when she came across Ian on the park bench. She walked over to say hi.

"Fancy meeting you here; are you out for one of your jogs?"

"I don't jog. I run," was his snippy reply.

"Yeah, sorry you did say run. I'm just enjoying the beautiful day. Isn't it nice?"

"I hadn't noticed. Hey I am going to take off. Bye."

Symone didn't know what to make of his shortness. They had conversed so easily camping, and at the coffee shop and even at the zoo yesterday. She didn't want to take it personally. She couldn't think of anything she had done to upset him. She headed home and took a shower. Usually a shower made everything better. It didn't this time. She was really enjoying being his friend and didn't like the vibe she got today.

On the other side of town

Ian realized that he had been a jerk. He didn't want company today because of the bad mood dealing with Jimmy's mom had put him in. She never used to give him trouble about seeing him. It was making him insecure about his position in Jimmy's life. He was always at her mercy, since Jimmy lived with her. Now she was making him feel he was at her mercy and that didn't sit well.

He picked up his phone and droplets of water from his hair dripped on his phone but he didn't care.

"Sorry I was short earlier."

There was no response because Symone was having a movie day with Kat and didn't look at her cell phone until she was turning off the alarm in the morning.

She noticed the message and told herself she would reply when she got to work. However, an important message at work distracted her and she got caught up in her work until a bouquet of roses showed up.

"Delivery for Symone Watkins"

"That's me," she smiled as she accepted the flowers.

She read the card and smiled. She sat them down on her desk and picked up her cell phone and dialed.

"Hello"

"Hi, I just wanted to say thanks for the flowers."

"Oh, you're welcome. Now I know how many flowers it takes for you to accept my apology," he said hoping she could hear his smile through the phone. She could

"I haven't accepted it, yet, this is just how many flowers it takes to get my attention."

"I see how it is. I wondered after I didn't get any response to my text.

"Movie marathon, I'm sorry. I didn't see it until this morning"

Both content that they were back to conversing easily, they made plans for lunch the following day. Since he worked mostly from home they had arranged for her to pick him up. Symone walked up to his door the following day and rang the doorbell.

"Come in." she hears from inside.

She opens the door and enters.

"Hey, I will be right there. I'm just finishing up an edit to a picture."

Symone took in the room. The only décor were his pictures. On the in-table by the couch was a picture of Jimmy with a poem or story inset in the other half of the frame. She picked it up and read.

My Greatest Love/Fear

I thought I knew myself
But the day you came into the world
Everything changed.

Power didn't have a definition
Before I felt these emotions

I had never known love
Love so strong it can't be killed

I had never known fear
Fear so strong it can cripple
Nothing was ever so intimidating
As the love and I fear
For you Little Man

She wiped her moist eyes and realized she hadn't heard Ian walk into the room.

"My brother tried to revoke my man card for writing that. I said I should revoke his for framing it for everyone to see."

"What an adorable baby he was." She said while laughing at the brotherly antics.

"Thanks, I think so. Shall we??"

Symone allowed herself to be directed back to the car and to lunch. They enjoyed a nice lunch and the rest of the afternoon all Symone could think of was that she now knew him better. She had been embarrassed to be caught reading the poem, but he had been just as embarrassed for the vulnerability it displayed. She hadn't wanted to embarrass him further by drawing attention but she was greatly intrigued by his writing.

Ian did what he usually did when he missed Jimmy. With beer in one hand and Jimmy's picture in another he sat down on the couch to brood. Although the time with Symone had one much to improve his mood, he was surprised to admit, he still didn't feel easy with the situation.

Chapter 4 – Comfort and an Intervention

Ian found he was happy that he got to see more of Symone. He wouldn't think about how happy or why but that was beside the point. He wasn't happy however with not getting to see Jimmy. In fact he was about the pick up the phone and talk to Jimmy's mother about spending some extra time with him when his phone buzzed. It was his brother.

"What's up?" was his cheerful greeting from his brother.

"Work, you know how it is." Ian responded

"I do know. That is why I called. All work and no play, so I am taking you out this weekend. I found this new club. You are going to love it."

"I doubt it. You know that's not my thing. Count me out." Ian responded, knowing his brother wouldn't let him off the hook easily.

"Count you in. Ok. Perfect. You want me to pick you up?" came the persistence Ian expected.

"You heard me punk." Ian said trying to sound final

Better a punk than an old man, I know you're my big brother. Really you can stop "setting the example" and let loose."

"Who are you calling old man?" Ian said with a chuckle.

"You, Old Man. Come on, what can happen"

"What can happen indeed? Did you forget TJ?"

"Man I paid back the bail money. That is water under the bridge. Besides this is not Mexico."

Ian did not feel like he lived a stodgy life. He traveled and had the unconventional job after all. Nothing could make him feel like a prude like his brother. A freer spirit was never born. Free spirit, who was he kidding, a more reckless person was never born. It was almost as if the fact that Ian always protected his brother gave his brother Jace the license to be reckless. On the other hand, Jace never hurt anyone with his antics, and he was someone who always had his back. He hardly ever said no to Jace.

"Dude, I was just going to call to make plans to see Jimmy this weekend."

"Come with me this weekend and I promise I will call and get you Jimmy time for the next two weekends. Old Man"

"Ok, just to shut you up." Ian finally relents.

"You won't regret it."

"Oh I probably will, but I'm in anyway."

The next morning saw Symone on the phone with her father.

"Good Morning, sweetie."

"Good Morning, dad."

"Happy Mother's Day"

"Happy Mother's Day, Dad can I ask you a question?"

"Of course"

"I know you love Kathy but, do you still think about her?"

There was an excessively long pause and then:

"Yes, Every day. When I hear your voice right now, it makes me think of her. But if you tell Kathy, I will deny it."

Symone let out a long sigh she hadn't realized she'd been holding and giggled at his attempt at levity

"Honey I love you. Shoot that's the other line. It is probably one of your sisters."

"Ok Dad. I love you two. Give Kathy a hug and kiss for me."

"Ok. Bye sweetie."

"Bye"

She pulled a blanket from the cabinet and with a glass of wine curled up on the couch for her favorite movie, Pride and Prejudice. She was on her second glass of wine and the third episode of the movie when there was a knock on the door.

"Did I get you out of bed?" asked Ian commenting on her pajamas and disheveled hair

"Nope, this is my Friday off and I just never got out of them today. I should be embarrassed today but I'm really not. Come in though."

"There's nothing wrong with that. Oh and I come bearing gifts." He holds a package that Symone just realized he had in his hands.

"For me, why thank you. Let's see what it is."

She rips it open and discovers a framed copy of the picture from the camping trip that would shortly be featured on the magazine cover.

"Oh how beautiful. I think what you did the lighting enhanced that sunset and I honestly didn't think that was possible."

"Nah, I just capture what is already there" was his modest reply.

She looked at him and tried to decide if it was false modesty or sincere humility. He didn't have a smirk or smile as if he expected the praise so she decided on humility. This analysis distracted her from the fact that her eyes were feeling up with tears.

"Hey, what is wrong" he asked with a voice full of concern.

"Oh don't mind me. I am just being a crybaby girl."

"I doubt that. We are friends right. You can tell me, unless you don't want to talk about it."

"It's Mother's Day."

Ian instantly understood. His mother left him and Jace but he still missed having one. He reached out encircled her in his arms and held her there for a few seconds.

"I'm sorry to be such a Debbie Downer."

"I'm sorry that here when you need someone to comfort you, there is only me. I'm sure you'd much rather one of your sisters was here right now. Don't let me overstay my welcome. Ok."

"Actually, I don't feel I can talk to Kat or Raven about this because I think they feel it detracts from their mom. Dad is the only one who understands but he doesn't want to make his wife feel bad talking about her."

"I didn't think of it like that, but that makes sense. Well let me make myself useful and refill that glass of yours."

"You're my guest I should be getting you one."

"Oh I'm not going to let you drink by yourself trust me my friend."

To which she only smiled and indicated what cabinet he could find the wine glasses in. He quickly returned with two glasses of wine.

"So, what are we watching?"

"Pride and Prejudice"

"Can't say I've ever watched it but I'll give it a shot."

"Honestly, I don't know that I was watching it. It was just noise."

"Well then tell me about your mom"

So she told her how much her mom loved the beach and about how she made ceramics. She told him how her mother's hair was so incredibly long she had to keep care she wouldn't burn it when cooking.

She described the memories and feelings of events but how her voice and even some of her features were fading. She shared the picture of her mother in the locket she always wore. He didn't comment on how much like her mother she looked, she probably got that a lot. She didn't have to say the words to convey the loneliness of carrying the memories of her mother by herself.

"I feel guilty. I look at her picture just to remember. I don't have a voice recording to remember her voice though" she said almost in tears.

"It doesn't seem to me you don't have anything to feel guilty about. You honor her memory by keeping it safe in your heart."

"So tell me about your mom. You did say something about the other half of your life story didn't you?" she asked drowsily.

"Half a life story I did mention but my mom? I think that would ruin mother's day. We'll save that for another time."

"Ok, another time," was Symone's half sleeping response.

They had scooted closer to each other on the couch during their conversation and so as she became drowsier her head fell on his shoulder. The movie was over and the wine glasses were empty so she scooped her up and carried her into her bedroom and gently laid her on the bed. He took her shoes off and laid them beside her. He was about to leave but right as he turned away she became disturbed and began fidgeting and reached out and took his arm and said:

"No"

He knew she was asleep but she kept fidgeting so he just sat down on the edge of the bed and held her hand. When, maybe because she was deeper asleep, she released his hand he returned to the living room, kicked his shoes off and wrapped up in the blanket and fell asleep on the couch. He just couldn't bring himself to leave her alone tonight.

When he awoke the next morning he could hear her in the kitchen. As if he summoned her she appeared in the doorway.

"Can I interest you in some coffee? It's the least I can do for my friend that listened to me carry on all night."

"Got any hot chocolate? And I would hardly say you carried on."

"Hot chocolate it is. And thank you, for the gift and listening to me."

She finished making the beverages and came out with the coffee, his hot chocolate and English muffins. They talked about work, interests, anything other than mothers. As time usually did between them, it passed fast and all of the sudden it was late morning.

"Well, thank you for breakfast. I better head out if I want to fit a run and shower in before I have to meet Jace."

"Oh yeah, well, thank you again." Symone said with a self-conscious smile.

The next few weeks became a blur for the both of them. The lunches that were quickly becoming a habit became hit and miss. Without the lunch to break up her day Symone did as she always did and buried herself in her work, unless Kat or Raven dragged her away. Ian didn't like the club scene but Jace was insistent. More to the point, he felt he had to save Jace from himself. So when Ian's phone buzzed this morning and Jace's pictured appeared on the caller idea, he thought he knew what to expect.

"Good Morning. Monday is a little early in the week to be planning for the weekend even for you."

"Good Morning. Hey, so I talked to Jimmy's mom like I promised to. You need to call her she has news for you."

"What news," Ian was immersed in work and not in the mood for riddles.

"Just call her."

"Ok"

They hung up and Ian called her. She indicated that she needed to hear it in person. Symone was concentrating her work so hard that the beep of her phone startled her.

Can't do lunch today. Something came up Dinner? – Ian

She typed back:

I can't tonight. Working late. Thursday? I'll drive? – Symone

Her phone beeped

Sure. See you then.

Thursday evening came quickly for Symone. It saw her working all the way until dinner time. She had stolen away for a quick break and in the window of one store had seen a stuffed monkey she had to have for Jimmy. She picked up her present and drove to Ian's house to pick him up.

"Who is it?" was the response when she rang the doorbell.

"Symone, did you forget about dinner?"

There was no response except for the door finally opening and what Symone saw when it opened broke her heart. Ian was sobbing uncontrollably even though he was making visible attempts to stop. She asked him what was wrong and he couldn't respond. His phone began ringing, seeing that he was in no shape to talk she took the initiative to answer and he attempted a grateful smile.

"Hello, this is Ian's phone."

"Hey. This is Jace. Is he ok?"

"Jace this is a friend, Symone. No he's not ok. Are you able to come over?"

"No, I've got a gig. I didn't want him to be alone so I was going to talk him into coming to see it whether he felt like it or not. I guess he told you what happened?"

"Well no, he hasn't been able to."

Jace proceeded to inform her about his conversation with Jimmy's mom. She had told him she suspected Jimmy wasn't Ian's kid. Apparently Ian immediately demanded a blood test and the lab had just called that day and confirmed the worst.

"My brother didn't want to be a father yet. He always had me to look out for, that was quite enough let me tell you. I can't say the words for what that woman is. She trapped him with the pregnancy. Probably because she knew he would step up and try to do the right thing by his son. And he has. I'm so glad someone is with him. Tell him I will be by in the morning"

I will. Bye Jace."

Bye"

She put the phone down, closed the door behind her and threw her arms around Ian.

OMG, I am so sorry Ian."

He's not mine," was all he could say.

He allowed her to guide him to the couch. They both sat down and he proceeded to crumble. She could see the heartbreak in his eyes and in his voice.

She knew too; or at least suspected. She named him after the guy of all things," he said bitterness accompanying the grief.

You're sure. Jace mentioned a blood test?" she asked.

He pointed with his head to the table and she picked up the paper there. She read the bad news for herself and put it down as if it was dangerous in and of itself.

I'm sorry is so inadequate. I wish there was something I can do."

What's in the bag?"

She was equally surprised because she had forgotten about the present in her hand and surprised that he registered its existence right now at all.

Oh. I saw this and just had to have it for Jimmy," she says sheepishly as she reluctantly pulls it out.

It's perfect. She said I can see him one more time to say goodbye. Gracious of her right? You should go with me and give it to him then."

If you want, I'd be happy to," was her only response. She was without words, and couldn't comprehend inflicting this kind of pain.

He reached to his right and picked up the picture of Jimmy.

What do I do with this? I can't get rid of it, but I can't look at it," he said. The words expressed the loss mirrored in his eyes and face.

"No, don't get rid of it. I think you should find a safe place where you don't have to at it but think you will regret it if you get rid of it."

He looked at it and lovingly ran his fingers over the picture and then cradled it to his chest and just sighed. He looked at her but she could tell he didn't see her. He didn't see anything but Jimmy and the pain. She had been holding his hand but released to go to the refrigerato and brought him back a beer. He took it and looked her with gratitude but it went unspoken. Their ease of conversation had transformed into something more. She sat down beside him and looped her arm through his and they sat that way for a long while. Sometimes they talked and sometimes they didn't. At one point of silence he laid his head on her lap and she took to stroking his head and the both dozed off and on

She finally noticed that darkness overtook the room. She got up to turn on a lamp and saw that he was asleep. He allowed her to direct him to bed and she rendered him the same service she had received on Mother's Day.

She went to get up a short time later and realized he held her wrist. He was sound asleep with one hand around the picture and one on her wrist. The movement caused him to stir, but instead of waking up he put down the picture and tugged her yet closer. She tried to wriggle free but his grip got tighter and his eyes fluttered open and she heard:

"Please. Don't Leave"

She was leaning on the picture now so she picked it up, laid it on the in table. She then lay down beside him on the bed and watched him sleep. She snuggled down to be supported by the headboard and pillows. She brushed some bangs out of his face and closed her eyes and that is the last thing she remembered.

Ian awoke to the faint smell of soap and water. He opened his eyes and saw Symone wrapped in his arms. He remembered faintly being led to bed but beyond that nothing. He saw how he held her wrists and released them instantly. He watched her sleeping and was overwhelmed with emotion. Gratitude for her care and comfort, and something else he couldn't describe. She wasn't exactly beautiful, but there was something about her contradicting combination of inner strength and vulnerability. He was extremely drawn to it in a way and to such an extent he didn't understand. He ran the back of his palm down her cheek and gently kissed her forehead. That was when he noticed she wasn't wearing the locket with her mother's picture.

He sighed and rolled onto his back and instantly felt bereft. He vaguely remembered asking her to stay. He chocked it up to the situation with Jimmy. He wasn't ready to admit to any feelings, he couldn't contemplate the implication at a time like this. He decided to go take a shower hoping it would help him gain control of his emotions.

Symone awoke because she was suddenly cold when she had been warmer all night than she ever remembered. She heard him in the shower, and decided she needed coffee.

Ian came out of the bathroom in his shorts to find an empty apartment. When he walked into the living room he found a post it on the television indicating she would return momentarily, she was just on a coffee run.

Again, as if she could be conjured by his thoughts, she walked through the door.

She gave him the hot chocolate she had bought him and started to make a comment about coffee making her feel more of a human but then decided feeling like a human wasn't in the cards right now.

The peace and quiet that had descended upon them while they sipped their beverages was disturbed by the entrance of Jace.

"Good Morning," Jace greeted them both. Symone could tell the concern in his look when he tried to assess how his brother fared.

"Good Morning," they returned in unison.

"You must be Symone," was his enthusiastic introduction.

She nodded her response. She suddenly felt out place. She rose and said:

"Well, I need to get to work, but" she looked at Ian "let me know the plan."

He nodded while tipped his hot chocolate and with that she was gone. Symone didn't know why she went to work; her only thoughts were of Ian and his situation. She had received a text indicating that his visit with Jimmy was this evening and that her company was still desired.

Back at the apartment

"What plan? Are we getting revenge?" Jace asked while proceeding to call Jimmy's mom every derogatory term in his arsenal.

"You're not helping," Ian indicated "and no she only meant the plan for the final visit with Jimmy" Ian almost choked on how bad the word final tasted in his mouth.

The brothers argued over the proposed course of action to get over this grief. Jace proposed partying with him and Ian, while it was one of the last things he wanted to do, didn't have the drive to resist his charismatic and persistent sibling.

Symone kept in touch with Ian over the following weeks but was getting discouraged because for some reason he seemed to be dodging her. The only times she had seen him was the visit with Jimmy and once for lunch where he had given her a new chain for her mother's locket. She thought about how touched, not just by the gift itself, but that he had noticed it was missing. Not that him being thoughtful was remarkable but he had noticed while undergoing a very difficult time itself. That pleasant memory was replaced by her discomfort about his demeanor lately. Not only had she perceived him to be dodging her but he was very distant when she called or texted.

One such Saturday when these thoughts were plaguing her she attempted to put them out of her mind. She took a long walk, and decided to do some shopping for the big trip to see their mom and dad. The grueling task of trying on clothes for a woman with body issues did much to distract her mind from Ian but that was only temporary. When it was evening and she still looked for distraction she was about to call Raven or Kat when her phone buzzed

"Hello"

"Symone?" came a slurred voice through the phone.

"Ian?" she didn't question that it was him but was surprised to hear him drunk.

"I-i-i can't find my keys and Jace can't drive. Can you come get me?"

"Yes, where are you?"

She listened to the address of the club they were at and headed out. Equal parts annoyed and worried warred for space in Symone's mind. She got to the club and when she saw that he was very drunk but unharmed annoyed won out.

"Let's go boys," she said as she led Jace and Ian out to the car. She asked Jace if she was taking him home or to his brothers and he indicated he wanted to go home. She then became exceedingly curious about how Ian had gotten into this situation and since Jace seemed much less affected by the drink she directed her questions to him.

"I thought it would be good for him, especially since the thing with Jimmy," Jace offered in response to her question.

"This has happened before? How did you guys get home then?" more horrified by the thought they might have driven like this than anything else.

"We usually have company; and they take us to pick up our cars the next day."

She helped Ian in the house and to bed which was no small feat. The fact that his legs weren't working well made drunken weight almost as difficult to manage as dead weight. Symone was significant smaller than him but the anger that was welling up inside her gave her strength beyond normal.

He huffed out a breath when she plopped him on the bed and the smell of alcohol invaded Symone's breathing space. She went to his dresser and doused him with cologne to cover the smell. She covered him up and went to make her a bed on the couch. The fact that she was mad didn't make her less concerned for him. In fact, her anger turned inward because she knew very well she was being fanciful and didn't really believe their friendship would progress further. Her anger dissipated further when her inner thoughts turned to concern that his grief for Jimmy would turn into self-destructive behavior.

When Ian awoke the next morning he couldn't remember how he got home. He staggered into the living room and saw the answer sleeping peacefully on the couch. He took in the peaceful demeanor on her sleeping face and cringed at what must have been going through her mind when she had gotten his call last night. For the life of him though he couldn't figure out why he smelled *so* strongly of cologne.

Symone awoke to the smell of coffee. She opened her eyes and there was a Starbucks sitting in front her as it was an offering saying, I'm sorry. She heard the shower and pulled the blanket around her shoulders and waited for him to get out. He walked into the living room in shorts and while toweling his head and joined her on the couch, but said nothing. After an interminable silence:

"So do you want to talk about it?" she asked attempting nonchalance.

"Not really, but I don't see how I am going to get out of it," was his grumpy response.

"Jace said he talked you into it but is this really how you want to deal with it," she said more acerbically than she intended.

"I am a grown man, responsible for my own actions. Jace doesn't talk me into anything and I really don't need you judging me."

She got up, anger and hurt and disappointment clearly expressed in her posture, face, and tone:

"I know you're a grown man. I wasn't trying to be judgmental. I was just concerned for a friend who appears to not want concern so I can only be disappointed I wasted my time."

Just like that she was gone and just like that his pique turned to guilt.

Symone got home and in all the commotion realized she had left her phone in the car. Upon retrieving it she found several missed calls from Kat so she decided to call her.

"Hey you I started to worry, where have you been?" asked Kat.

"Don't ask."

But her sister could hear the emotion in her voice and came over. They shared a glass of wine and Symone told her how she was concerned that Ian was partying to cover up the pain from something difficult he was going through without divulging Ian's privacy. Kat swallowed her surprise over how close her sister and Ian had apparently became.

Symone had to admit talking with her sister had made her feel better. They said good night early because it was a work night. In fact, she had just said goodbye to Kat when her doorbell rang

"Did you forget something?" she asked. Only it wasn't Kat.

"Yes, my manners. Can you accept my apology?" he asked not only with his words but his eyes.

"Yes, but you can't be pushing me away and being a jerk every time things are rough. If we're going to be friends you have to accept that I'm going to be concerned about you."
"You're right. Being alone, just Jace and I, I kind of made pushing people away my modus operandi. If you're willing to be patient and give me another chance I promise to work on not pushing you away."

She smiled brightly and that was that. She then noticed the large bag in his hand and he indicated it was a gift. It turned out to be a coffee pot.

"Thanks but I have a coffee pot already."

"Not at my house. These overnighters are becoming a habit, and yes I know how that sounds but you know what I mean. Anyway I just figured this was save the coffee runs."

"You think I can be bought with coffee huh."

"Yeah I figured out how many flowers to get your attention, and there's been enough coffee runs to know how important it is so I figured it might get one at least a shot at forgiveness.

That caused them both to laugh and with that a new understanding was born. With very few exceptions Ian didn't give her cause for concern anymore. On those few occasions when she did get those calls on a Saturday night, Symone reasoned that if a few nights to numb the pain were what he needed she wouldn't complain.

Chapter 5 – Friendship is Tested

The time came for the trip to South America for Symone and her sisters to visit their parents. Life was good. Ian and Symone were supposed to have lunch the day before the trip but plans changed. However, Symone felt confident that he was going to eventually be ok. The three sisters made plans to stay together so they would all make it to the airport on time. Before she leaves for her sister's house she called Ian just to say good bye, and:

"Hello" came a syrupy sweet female voice through the phone.

"Hi, I might have the wrong number," Symone said

"Well, who you calling honey?" the syrupy sweet voice returned.

"Ian"

"You got the right number but he's in the shower, can I take a message?"

"Yes can you tell him Symone just called to say hi?"

"I will, sweetie. Anything else?"

"No"

Symone hung up and was instantly happy she was leaving the country. She didn't know what was going on but she was glad to have a week to figure how she felt and to avoid overreacting. She felt hurt, disappointed, and overall just plain wretched but she put on a brave face for everyone's sake. The last thing she wanted was to be questioned about it and have to talk about it before she was sure of her own feelings.

The plane ride was bearable only with cocktail. Raven was her usually bubbly self. Symone loved her sister and would do anything for her, but the mood that one phone call had put her in found that effervescence intolerable for the time being. Things improved significantly when they arrived. She found she could hibernate by the pool and beach. Not much was asked of her. This was good because she wasn't capable of much, evidence of just how dismal her spirits were.

It was the last day of the trip. It was on one such occasion she was sitting on in a recliner by the pool when someone suddenly casting a shade caused her to look up:

"Hey dad"

"Mind if I join you?" he asked.

"Please" she completed her acceptance by motioning to a nearby recliner. She went back to reading her book though

"So, are you going to tell me what's bothering you, or do I have pull it out of you as a dentist does teeth as per usual."

"What makes you think something is a matter?" was her weak attempt at deflection.

"Just who exactly think you're trying to fool young lady. If I can't tell something is wrong with you who can. It's a man isn't it?"

She tried to hide the surprise that he hit the mark. She didn't succeed.

"His name is Ian" she began.

While omitting his personal business concerning Jimmy she went on to tell her dad about the strange camping trip they met on. She explained how close she felt they had become. His kindness on mother's day, being there for him during a difficult situation he was going through and then the woman answering his phone and how bad that had felt.

"Do you love him?"

"WOW dad, get right to the point?"

"Well my dear what else matters?"

"I don't know you tell me?"

"No I asked the question first"

"I have no idea. I can't say I've been in love before so how am I supposed to know. Even if I do, is it worth all this trouble?"

"Let me tell you something. After your mother I thought love was impossible. I would never love again, so I gave up hope and didn't try. I only began trying again when I found love again. I made many mistakes trying to find it again but never did I stop looking for it. So is it the worth the trouble? I say yes, it's the only thing that is."

She thought about her father's words. They had already been through a lot together in a short time. She knew that she valued his opinion. She knew that enjoyed time with him, cared about him, worried about him. Did she love him though?

Symone found the return trip more than bearable and was even able to join in her sister's exuberance. She was through baggage claim and her phone came alive with signal and beeped.

Have a good trip?

To which we responded:

Very nice. How did you know I was back?

Beep

I have my spies. LOL Brian heard from Kat.

Another beep

Can we talk?

She slowly typed back

S-U-R-E

Another beep

Ok, I will come over

She didn't know why she was so hesitant to see him. Maybe he just wanted say hi. The truth was she was scared to see him. Afraid she wouldn't like what she found out when she asked about the girl who answered his phone.

He was waiting on her doorstep when she got home from the airport. He followed her in and she divested herself of her luggage and he gave her a big hug.

"I've missed you Breezy," was his casual greeting

"Oh" she said not sure whether to be relieved or disappointed, "Hi. When you asked to talk I thought it might be more serious than saying hi."

"I do have news" he replied

"Oh" she ventured. She was still unsure if she wanted to hear it.

"I've been seeing someone," he said hesitantly

"I know" she replied

"You do?"

"Yeah I called you before my trip and she answered," she admitted "I take it she didn't tell you I called."

"No, she must have forgot"

Symone was sure she hadn't forgotten and had purposely not told him. Ian, strangely enough, seemed buoyed by her knowing the news and continued:

"There is more. We got married this weekend," he said with eyes cast to the floor like he couldn't look at her.

To say the world crumbled beneath her at that moment would be an understatement. She wished she could be devoid of all emotion; that the earth would swallow her up then and there. She knew right then and there that she loved him and she wished she didn't. It wouldn't hurt nearly so much if she didn't.

"That is a little sudden right?" she asked without knowing how she formed the words.

"A little" he ventured

"Congratulations I guess."

"That wasn't close to being convincing. I admit to being a little drunk when it happened and I would feel a lot better about things if I knew you were ok with it."

For some reason that made the all the pent up emotion come rushing forth

"What am I supposed to say? Am I supposed to reassure you that you made the right decision? Do you even love her? Who does this?"

Fortunately the couch was there to break her fall because, completely spent by all the emotion, she collapsed to the couch after her outburst. He slowly approached, sat down and took her in his lap and stroked her hair.

"You have to believe the LAST thing on this earth I wanted to do was hurt you" he took a breath "Do I love her? No I don't want to love anyone. I married her in part because I don't love her. It's better that way. I doubt she loves me either. She doesn't have to strip while she's married, I'm sure that was reason enough for her."

At that Symone raised her head

"She's a stripper?"

"Was"

"Ok, First of all I don't buy for one minute that you don't love anyone. I have seen you with Jimmy and Jace so I know that's a lie. I can only think that you want to spare my feelings from the reality that you aren't attracted to me. Well I want to hear it, I want to hear you say it" she was almost screaming the last part.

"No, you won't ever hear me say that because it is not the truth," he said in such calm the contrast to her angst was not lost on either of them "You are attractive. Why would you even think you aren't?"

"Because that is how it has always been. They think of me as a friend, sister but nothing more. I'm unlovable."

"Seriously? I just had the biggest argument with my brother because when he walked in and saw you in my apartment but found out we weren't intimate he wanted a chance. I almost killed him."

"That was just a territorial thing, doesn't make me loveable. My dad married so many times and it's not because of him, after all he loved me mom and he loves Kathy. It was them."

"With all due respect to your dad it was wrong of him to make mistakes that would leave you with that complex. He did something right because you are an amazing person through and through. You just don't understand. If anything you are too good for me."

"You're right I don't understand. I'm too good for you? What? Make me understand?"

"How can I make you understand my mom? She was a really good mom until after Jace was born. She told me one day that there was one of her and two of us so I needed to be a good boy and make it easy on her. One day I got in trouble at school and she had to leave work to deal with it. The next day she lost her job. After that, she was different, like she no longer cared about anything. She wouldn't change Jace's diaper or cook dinner and it just got worse until she ended it. She never said it but I know it's my fault. When things happened with Jimmy it was like God telling me I was right about that so I didn't deserve Jimmy"

When Symone looked in his eyes she only saw the little boy who lost his mommy. It was her turn to try to dispel his demons or at least kick them out of the room for the moment.

"Ian that simply isn't true. I'm sure that single incident didn't cost your mom's job. I'm sure there's more to the story of your mom, depression probably for years. Most importantly though, I believe with all my heart God would never put someone through the pain that your situation with Jimmy caused you. He's a loving God, he wouldn't do that. It's just a case of a manipulative, desperate woman."

"Well you got Jimmy's mom pegged for sure."

She was calm enough to notice now that she was on his lap and went to get up but he held her close.

"I didn't know your mom but I know women. It sounds like your mom might have had postpartum depression. You couldn't have changed anything. She would have needed medical or other professional help"

He didn't look any more convinced he hadn't been the cause of his mother's troubles than she was she was loveable

"So what now?" he asked

"I suspect your wife must be wondering where you're at."

"Nah, she is out of town for the weekend. I am not leaving until everything is ok here."

"Well I don't know about you but I'm exhausted and it's late" she said suddenly anxious for him to be gone.

"Are we ok though? Are you ok?"

"I am and we are. Let me know when I can meet your bride."

He looked at her with skepticism but gave her a hug and said his good bye. Symone went to bed exhausted and cried herself to sleep. She awoke the next morning feeling as if she had een run over by a truck. She could only give thanks that is was her favorite day of the week, unday. She made coffee and immediately made herself comfortable on the couch. She had lecided to allow herself one day of brooding and then she would get on with life. She ignored er phone except for family. She turned on a movie but it wasn't even registering as ackground noise. Her thoughts repeatedly went to Ian and the change in their situation. he doubted herself as she thought back to her feeling that there had been a connection. lowever, when she thought about the vulnerable moments they had shared even when they irst met and spent the night stuck on the cliff she didn't think she could be imagining it ither. There was so much that she wanted to say and yet of what benefit would it be.

t boiled down to one of two options. Either she would continue to be his friend, and include is wife in that sphere and relationship or distance herself from him and in effect cut off the elationship. Her breath hitched and she instantly dismissed the idea of ending the elationship. He had already become such a significant figure to her that she didn't want to ose that.

ymone awoke the next morning with fresh eyes and renewed spirit. The determination to iccept the situation as it was and the power that that decision had ultimately been hers to nake left her in a good frame of mind. Her determination faltered some when she got the ext from Ian asking if they were still on for their weekly lunch date. It only did so emporarily though, and she replied in the affirmative. That didn't keep lunch from starting ut awkwardly silent.

Ok, it won't do for us to sit here and say nothing" she said, finally ending the silence.

Yeah I know I'm still trying to figure out if you're mad though" was his sheepish response.

I wasn't mad, surprised definitely. Besides we didn't make any promises. I don't have a eason to be mad."

True, it appears I have to be drunk to make anyone any serious promises,"

ymone choked on her drink when she heard this. She couldn't suppress a chuckle but at east had to good form not to comment on how badly that boded for his marriage.

Why do you think that is?"

I don't know, commitment phobic, pick your stereotype" was his flip response.

Sure, well I know the truth. You forget we talked about part of it the other night. It's much nore than that."

Maybe" was his vague acknowledgement "I'm just glad we're past the awkwardness and can be riends and most importantly, you're still talking to me. I would hate to lose your friendship."

"I hope we can always be friends and it's nice to hear our friendship is important to you."

"It's more important than you know."

Symone excused herself because her lunch break was over but not before encouraging Ian to bring his wife to lunch next time. So he did. In fact, sometimes Ian wouldn't make lunch and it would be just him and his wife. Symone found her funny and good company and even helped Ian introduce her to their mutual friends. Conversation came inevitably to their whirlwind romance and then Symone found herself offering to plan a belated bridal shower.

Symone preceded Raven in walking in her apartment after the get together and announcement and Raven didn't so much as let the door shut before she let her sister know her opinion on the matter:

"You're throwing that woman a bridal shower, you?" she asked with the most incredulous look on her face.

"I throw great parties, why not?" Symone replied

"You know very well what I'm talking about. Everyone thought someone was going on between you and Ian and then he turns up married. If that's not weird enough, you offer to throw her a shower."

"It's not so weird. I was the first to meet her, and it will help the rest of our friends get to know her."

"You got to meet her first because of your relationship with Ian and no one knows her because it was out of nowhere. I can't believe you are as calm about this as you seem."

"I wasn't at first, I was plenty upset. I just decided that being his friend was more important than whether we had a romantic relationship or not and I think he feels the same way."

"So you're really ok?"

"I am"

The two sisters then enjoyed a glass of wine and watched a movie and talked no more of Ian, much to Symone's relief.

LOVE HOPES ALL THINGS

The day of the bridal shower came and went and was a great success. Ian and Symone found life kept them very busy and lunch dates became more and more infrequent, weeks went by and one or the other would have to cancel for one reason or another. Finally, Kat and Brian were hosting a dinner at Kat and Raven's house. Symone noticed Ian the moment she walked in the door, and he did her. He walked over to her:

"Hey stranger," he greeted.

"Hey back, how you doing?" she replied

"Not bad, what's new?"

"Nothing much, work still crazy busy. Where's your wife?"

"We're not together anymore."

"Wow I mean I knew I hadn't heard from her but I never expected. I'm so sorry," was her sympathetic response.

"I'm not. She cheated and lied about everything. I'm getting an annulment."

"How awful, honestly I'm sorry. I don't know what else to say."

"Really I'm fine. It was a stupid mistake in the first place, I regretted it almost immediately. I would have told you sooner but after such an idiotic move I didn't know . . . if I should."

"We were always friends right, of course you could tell me. I will always be here for you."

She put her arm through his to illustrate her point and then Brian's voice could be heard over everyone's.

"Can I have everyone's attention please?" he asked. And the room quieted down

"Thank You, we asked you all hear because we wanted to tell all of our loved ones and friends to know that Kat has agreed to make me the luckiest man alive and agreed to marry me."

The room erupted with cheers and applause and when Ian looked at Symone she had such a simply beautifully happy expression to her eyes, she looked truly beautiful. Ian and Symone wound their way through the crowd to the bride and groom.

"There is the maid of honor and best man" Ian greeted and slapped Ian on the back.

"I'm so glad you two are on good terms again, I was worried it would be weird to ask you two to stand up with us" Kat discreetly whispered into her sister's ear.

Symone's only response was to squeeze her arm.

The phone rang off the hook and the days ran together between normal work routine and helping Kat with preparations for the wedding. The lunches to discuss showers and decorations and dresses and photographers were never ending. It was especially fun when they would tie in their mother via face-time. It is understandable then that Symone was caught off guard and very much surprised when a co-worker Michael asked her out. She was so caught off guard she couldn't initially think of a response, so simply because she couldn't think of a reason to say no she found herself accepting the invitation.

Symone agreed to meet Michael at the restaurant they had agreed to for dinner. He was waiting for her outside, opened the door for her. He thanked her for agreeing to have dinner with him and indicated he had wanted to ask her out for a long time. She indicated her surprise at this but in the back of her mind knew her mind had been elsewhere even before the wedding preparations. He really seemed a nice guy and Symone was trying to talk herself into giving him a chance. All of a sudden a familiar voice:

"Fancy meeting you here," Ian said.

"Ian?" Symone said in surprise, "Michael, this is my friend Ian. Ian this is Michael, we work together."

"I was just leaving and thought I would say hi. You both enjoy your dinner. Symone" and with that he was gone.

Symone enjoyed the rest of the evening with Michael, friendly conversation and when he asked her if he could see her again at the end of the night she said yes with a light heart. She drove home and was walking up to her door, thinking about running into Ian when as if out of thin air he appeared in the light of her doorway.

"Hi, can we talk?"

"Sure, come on in."

They entered the house and she laid her scarf on the back of the couch and turned around to face him.

"What's up?"

"First of all, I admit I have no right to ask. . ."

"However you are asking anyway," she said, unaware and uncaring if she was cutting him off or saving him the trouble of having to voice the words.

His response came with the nod of his head.

'You're right you have no right to ask" was her response and she turned her back and headed to the kitchen to pour a glass of wine.

'It just took me by surprise," he said.

"I didn't know if would affect you at all, so I'm sorry" her acerbic, annoyed tone getting worse by the moment.

"You don't owe me an apology. In fact, I am well aware that you don't owe me anything. I just . . ." he faltered.

"You just, what? Ian, what do you want from me?" she asked, her defensive posture letting up.

"I just want things to go back to the way there were between us before."

"Then I suggest you take it up with the man in the mirror because I am not the ones that made things change. Talk about being taken by surprise. We opened up to each-other. I thought some kind of relationship was building and all of a sudden you turn up married. Now, you see me on a date and what, it bothers you?"

"Yes it bothers me" he said defensively.

He could tell this raised her hackles by the arched eyebrows and quickly set about changing his tone.

"That is my problem not yours though. The only thing that I want you to know is that I care about you, I always have. I think I always will."

"I care about you too" she replied.

"Are you serious about him?" he asked hesitantly

"It was our first date, I mean. He's nice. I can't think of any reason not to take him seriously. Can you?"

He thought of the night he had given her the news of his marriage and immediately felt regret at what he was expressing now. How could he make her feel bad for dating when after what he had done?

"No I cannot. I better go."

Before he could make it to the door he felt a small hand on his arm, stopping him. He turned around and she smiled at him.

"You don't have to go. Of course you get the couch. I think the couch has your name on it tonight, don't you?"

"As long as I don't have to make a coffee run in the morning the couch suits me just fine."

She had extended an olive branch and it had been accepted. She entered his arms to give him a hug and he closed them around her, neither one giving it up for a while. The talked for a while but Symone got tired and went to bed.

Ian was restless and rolled over towards the couch and got a small whiff of ocean. He opened his eyes and the scarf she had dropped on the couch made him smile. He must have fallen back to sleep because he was awoken by noises in the other room. He got up and the scene he came across tore at his heart. Symone was fidgeting and tossing back and forth and crying softly:

"Mom, Where is my mom?"

He didn't know what to do so when she rolled away from him he laid down beside her and folded his arms around her. Almost instantly she calmed. It was so significant and dramatic a calm she whimpered in relief. In spite of his concern it drew a small chuckle. The calm that ensued lulled him to sleep as he listened to the soft sound of her breathing.

She was surprised when she woke up in Ian's arms. She wondered why he wasn't on the couch but just as quickly forgot about it when she went to make coffee. However, when Ian walked in while she was making coffee, he said:

"Doesn't seem like either one of us slept well last night"

"What do you mean? Did you have trouble sleeping?"

"I am glad to hear that it didn't disturb you're sleep but yeah you were tossing and turning. Didn't you wonder why I was in there with you when you woke up?"

LOVE HOPES ALL THINGS

Oh no, I didn't wake you up did I?"

would ask if you're like that a lot but somehow I doubt you would know"

Actually, my sisters have mentioned it. They would tease me."

Man, look at the time. I have an early meeting with a magazine and you have work" he said. His cell phone had just buzzed a reminder of his appointment.

He kissed her on the forehead and wished her a good day and was out the door.

It surprised Symone not to hear anything else on the subject from Ian. It felt as if there was more to say although she couldn't for the life of her think what. It didn't come as a shock but some kind of weird coincidence when instead of the weekly lunch date with Ian she found herself out with Michael. The surprise came in the fact that she was having an enjoyable time and found herself asking him to be her date to Kat's wedding.

The more time went by, the less she heard from Ian. She found she didn't seem to miss it quite as keenly as she had in the past. It gave her more confidence in her decision to invite Michael to the wedding, and it felt good to be moving on. This feeling was reaffirmed when she ran into Jace one day and he alluded to the fact Ian had fallen back into the club and party scene. While her heart ached for his well-being she told herself it wasn't her problem. She'd have to be satisfied that she wasn't getting calls for ride home because he was so wasted.

Her sister's told her how ecstatic they were that she didn't seem caught in her all work and no play mode and attributed this to Michael. She didn't have the heart to point out that it was assisting with Kat's wedding plans that was keeping her busy and she had only seen Michael a couple of times.

Chapter 6 – Absence and Grief

The day of the wedding was upon them. Ian found himself meeting up with the groom, a very nervously excited groom.

Who is this? I'm sorry I thought this was my friend Brian's room?" Ian teased when he saw the sparkling groom.

Shut up fool and get in here. You don't look shabby yourself," was Brian's rejoinder.

Yeah we clean up well."

"Can you believe I'm doing this?" Brian asked with a smile that went to his eyes.

"No, not hardly! You look crazy happy though, I'm happy for you dude."

"Only thing that could make this better is if I could see my best man happy too."

"You know me, I am always happy. Seriously, I am looking forward to seeing everybody today. It feels like I've lost touch with my friends. Well not you but . . ."

Brian's smile lost some of its brightness, he almost went solemn.

"No, I know what you mean, and I know who you mean. Look, it's none of my business but I don't want you to be blindsided, she brought a date today."

Ian's stomach did a little flip and he wanted to give some flip response like pretend he didn't know who Brian was referring to, but his friend wasn't stupid. It also felt all kinds of wrong to be anything less than one hundred percent honest with him on his wedding day.

"I told you I'd lost touch" Ian said while attempting a smirk. He recovered and said, "We're being much too serious, today is your wedding day. Now knock it off, it's bad enough you gipped me out of throwing a bachelor party."

Brian was not completely convinced but decided to drop the subject and so they proceeded to the hall for the ceremony.

Ian smirked at his friend when he asked him for the umpteenth time if he had the rings. The idea of pretending he had lost them crossed his mind, but he just smacked him on the back and said:

"Relax, they're right here," while patting his chest pocket

People fussed over boutonnieres and the flowers and music but before they knew it Ian was standing beside Brian and the ceremony started.

The flower girl and ring bearer were adorable and the bridesmaids were next. Raven sauntered down the aisle with a confidence so incongruous to her pixie haircut and style that he had to stifle a slight laugh. He had just recovered and looked up when his breath hitched.

Symone walked down the aisle and Ian couldn't take his eyes off her. Her slight smile brightened eyes that were already the most expressive he'd ever seen. Her hair was pulled back in a loose bun with slight curls outlining her face. The dress hung to her perfectly, not snuggle, but close enough to leave just enough to the imagination. His throat grew dry and developed a lump. She walked with a grace that befit a tall model instead of her diminutive frame. He could sense that she felt beautiful. She didn't just look beautiful, she was breathtaking. When their eyes finally met, her smile changed into something he couldn't describe. He just knew he wanted to see it forever, but hide it away so it was for him alone. It made him feel something he didn't understand but that he felt all the way down to his toes.

The ceremony concluded and everyone found their way to the reception. Ian walked in and his eyes immediately started scanning the room without knowing who we was looking for. At least he wouldn't acknowledge who he was looking for. He found her with a group, smiling and talking and he smiled until he saw the guy next to her had his hand on the small of her back. He felt a rage he knew he wasn't entitled to but it was there anyway.

The dancing started and best man and maid of honor were supposed to join the bride and groom about half way through so Ian walked over to take Symone's hand and led to her to the dance floor. There was a long silence and then:

"Good to see you stranger," Symone tried for levity

"Good to see you, it has been a while hasn't it?" he replied with anything but levity. In fact, the huskiness in his voice both startled and fascinated.

"Where have you been keeping yourself?" she joked because she didn't know what to do with the intensity of the situation.

"Just keeping an eye on Jace seems like it's become a fulltime job."

"I ran into him the other day, he seems to be doing ok"

"Jace doing ok, yeah I guess. So, what's new with you beside the man with his hand all over you?"

He felt her startle and bristle and inwardly cringed because even if he had a right to be jealous, which he didn't, he knew this wasn't the way to handle those feelings.

"If I didn't know better, I'd say you sounded jealous. Good thing we both know better," she said the last part almost as a question.

"Yeah we know better."

The song ended meaning the dance was over. He reached down and kissed her near her ear and whispered,

"Be happy"

LOVE HOPES ALL THINGS

The kiss was so achingly tender and the whisper so soft the shiver she was left with was the only thing telling her it was real. She found herself back at her table without knowing how she got there. It wasn't until Michael asked her to dance that she snapped back. Or so she thought.

"This was a beautiful wedding, and you look gorgeous, if I haven't said so already."

"Yes, I am so happy for my sister. She really deserves this."

He kept talking but Symone did not hear him or the music they danced too. All she heard was the achingly tender sound of his breath on her ear and neck. His smell, soap and pine trees infiltrated her senses and wouldn't let go.

"Ian, can we not talk for a second?" she asked without realizing her mistake until . . .

"Michael," her partner said.

"What?" she asked with genuine confusion

"My name is Michael, but you called me Ian"

"I"

"Ian is the best man right?" Michael asked.

But she could not answer

"I'm sorry Michael, I'm sorry"

"Don't apologize, you told me you weren't ready for a relationship and I pushed. I am going to take off. I would offer you a ride unless I'm assuming you're duties as maid of honor aren't over."

"I'm the sister, are they ever?" she asked while offering a weak smile.

"Take care" he said while he kissed her hand and left.

Sheer willpower saw her through seeing off the newlyweds and she saw to the elder members of her family who had come from out of town. She was in a daze and so didn't notice when her dad approached and kissed her cheek

"You look tired honey; let us give you a ride home."

"No it's ok dad, Raven is driving me."

"Well get some rest, you look pale."

"I will"

She knew that a ride home with Raven without talking was too much to hope for so she stilled herself for the oncoming inquisition, but all that came was:

"Michael left early?"

"Yeah I think that's over. I mean he's a perfectly great guy but I just don't feel that connection you know," Symone said knowing how weak it sounded.

"I just want you to be happy."

Symone smiled, not just because of how sweet her sister was but because of how it reminded her of that confusing moment this evening.

"I know, I love you"

After a significant number of reassurances that she would be ok and didn't need her sister to keep her company she went inside and instead of hanging her coat in the closet flung in on the back of the couch and flopped on the couch. She had lain down and was dozing off when her doorbell rang.

She staggered to the door but what she saw when she opened it had her wide awake. Jace was holding Ian up and when Ian looked up at her he said:

"I don't want to be a stranger."

Symone shrugged her shoulders at Jace.

"I picked him up for the wedding and was trying to cheer him up. When it was time to go home he got belligerent and insisted I bring him here. I didn't know what else to do."

"Come in."

"I am sure he will be ok in the morning, I can come get him to get his car then if that's ok with you."

"Ok" because really what else could she say.

She watched as Jace laid him on the sofa she had just been sleeping on. He slipped out the door and Symone was left there watching Ian.

"I don't want to be a stranger Breezy"

He stretched like a cat and his hand found her coat and he brought it to his nose and sniffed and held the coat to his chest. She went to grab it to hang it up and he pulled it even closer. She sighed, covered him with a blanket and went to bed.

She awoke to an empty house and was trying to stifle and calm her disappointment that he left without a word when the door opened and he walked in wearing a brilliant smile.

"Good morning" he said brightly

"Good morning" she replied hesitantly, "I thought you left"

"That would be a lousy way to repay you putting up with me on your couch last night."

"Why were you on my couch last night?" Symone asked

"I don't know if it was the wedding or seeing you with that guys hand on you but I just missed you. You looked so good, you smelled so good. I know this is crazy and you're seeing someone else but there it is,"

"Yeah I'm seeing someone else. I don't know what to do with this information. I mean you act like and say that you don't want a relationship with me, only now that I've moved on you what, can't handle it?"

"I can handle it. I just didn't like how it felt."

"And how did it make you feel?"

"I'm just not sure I know. It's hard to describe. I didn't like someone else touching you. I know it's not fair. I should keep the feelings to myself. I don't mean to put this on you, but I thought I owed you an explanation."

You are right! It's not fair. I can't, no I don't want to do this back and forth thing you do. What do you want from me?" she slumped down to the couch a bundle of emotions. He sat down beside her and crushed her to his chest.

I can tell you what I want for you. I want you to be happy," he used his finger and thumb to lift her chin to look him the eyes. "I want to be the one who makes you happy."

But?" she asked because she knew there was one.

But I don't think I'm capable of it."

She scoffed because she that's what he said when he got married and she still didn't understand it.

Why is the idea of me moving on with Michael different than the women from the bar you bed?"

Because you are capable of having feelings for him and I am sure that I don't have feelings for them."

I'm not capable of anything. He broke up with me because I called him you. I was so filled with you I couldn't move forward. That isn't healthy though, we can't go on like this. Until you are ready for a full relationship I would ask that you don't express that you have feelings for me. You said you want me to be happy right?"

More than anything" he rose from the couch "If that would make you happy I can do that."

When she didn't respond he squeezed her hand, kissed her tenderly and left. To say that the next few weeks or months were difficult for Symone would be an understatement. Ian was keeping his distance, probably because he thought was what she wanted, and she hated it. She poured herself into her work until it worried her whole family. She could tell she had really worried them when she got a call from dad.

Hello honey."

Hi dad, how are you guys doing?"

I'm good"

Really? Because you can tell me if you're not."

"I said I'm fine dad. I don't need you checking on me just because Kat or Rav call and say whatever they've told you about me."

"They've told me that you are working yourself ragged, not eating. That you have lost weight."

"Dad I'm fine, really. I have had something on my mind that's been bothering me a lot but I don't want to talk about it. I didn't mean to worry anyone; I am over the not eating thing. I have an appetite again."

"Have you got any vacation time left? You can come down sit by the pool and you don't have to talk, Kathy will make your favorite foods when you're hungry. We'll just let you recharge."

"That sounds really tempting Dad, let me think about it and get back to you."

"Ok hun. Let me know?"

"Ok I will dad."

"And Symone?"

"Yes?"

"If you think I cannot tell that you're just patronizing me you would be mistaken. Please take care of yourself baby."

"I will dad."

She hung up feeling grateful for her family and guilty that she had given them cause for concern. So she set about to turn things around. She got more rest, tried to eat more, visit with her sisters, and even work a little less. Raven or Kat would have lunch with her every week. It helped. She still thought about Ian, more than she would like to admit, but it no longer felt as if a weight was on her heart. It no longer felt as if it was a labor just to breathe. She even started walking in the morning and wanted to work herself up to run. She was not interested in going to Dad and Kathy's in Mexico though, and she hated to disappoint her dad. She could tell that her improvements made him feel better and when she announced she wasn't coming he didn't press her.

During the same weeks/months Ian wasn't doing much better. Jace had called him to discuss his plans for the weekends and whether they would involve Ian or not.   When Ian gave a lackluster positive to joining Jace this weekend, he said:

"Don't say yes on my account. No one is twisting your arm."

"You know that is not my scene. You know I only go because . . . "

"Don't spout that crap about you going to protect me. No one needs you around raining on their parade. You were more fun when you were enjoying the company of the ladies. These last few months when you haven't . . ."

"Shut up, you don't know what you're talking about."

"I know I don't want you going if you're not into having some fun. I don't need a bodyguard."

"Fine"

Ian didn't know who hung up first. He was not sure what he was madder about. His brother being ungrateful or his bringing up that had given up women a few months ago. That made him mad because it made him think about her and he didn't want to think about her because it made it hard to do what she had asked him.

His disagreement with Jace did nothing to help his mood. He worked, and then he brooded. He ran and then he brooded some more. To say he was going through the motions would be understating the obvious. Saturday came when he normally would be going out with Jace he was in a particularly bad mood and had gone for a run. He returned feeling some better, so he took a bath and went to work on his latest magazine project until late into the night.

He awoke feeling much better the next morning feeling much better. He went to the kitchen and made himself a pot of coffee. The smell of coffee was permeating through his apartment when he wondered when he started making coffee for himself. That thought was interrupted by the ringing of his phone:

"Hello?"

"Hello, am I speaking with Mr. Ian Shale?"

"Yes"

"This is Dr. Michaels from Metro Hospital. Mr. Shale, I'm afraid I have some bad news about your brother Jace."

"What do you mean bad news?"

"He was in an accident last night, there was a lot of trauma to his head and I'm afraid he didn't make it."

Ian got off the phone and threw the coffee pot across the kitchen. He could still hear the sound of breaking glass and smell of burnt coffee when he came to later.
Symone was on her way to have breakfast with Raven. She opened the door to head outside and almost ran into Brian:

"Hey brother-in-law of mine, to what do I owe the honor of this visit?"

"Let's go inside."

He described how Jace was on his way home when some guys he apparently upset at the bar jumped him and beat him and left him to die. He described how he had heard about the accident, and when he went to check on Ian, Brian had found him passed out the floor. He described that Ian's state of mind only seemed to be declining and asked her help.

"No offense brother, but if he wanted me around why hasn't he called?"

"He doesn't call me either. He won't ask for help from anyone but especially not from you, not after. . ."

"What?" Symone asked, wondering if he knew about after the wedding.

"This is just me guessing because he is not forthcoming. But it doesn't take a genius to guess something went down between you two around that time. Whatever it was he just seems to think that he needs to give you some distance. You may have every reason to upset or more with him I don't know but I can't help but feeling that if anyone can help him it's you."

"I doubt I can do any good, but I will try."

"You're my favorite sister in law" he said has he hugged her

"Oh you are in so much trouble when I tell Raven you said that."

"You are just ornery enough to do that aren't you?"

"Get out of here.

Brian went to tell her when the funeral arrangements were and then did just that.

Symone sat in a daze on her couch and was only stunned out of her daze when there was a knock at the door. She should have known someone would come looking for her when she missed breakfast. So she called to the door:

"Come in Raven."

She told her sister about Brian's visit and what had happened to Ian's brother.

"I am sorry for Ian's loss, don't get me wrong. However I think Brian was wrong to impose on you about this. I know you guys care for each other, but I don't want you to relapse to the way you were after Kat's wedding."

"I won't Raven, I promise. If I need to talk I will come to you I promise. But I have to go to him, be there for him."

Ian sat in the chair waiting for the funeral to start but he wasn't aware of much around him. He should take his sunglasses off as he was indoors but he hadn't worn them for the sun. He vaguely registered Brian sitting down on his right side and then a song indicated the service was about to start. The funeral was about to start when he heard a voice beside him:

"Is this seat taken?" as she sat down beside him. Then she took his hand. His only response was a slight squeeze.

Her presence registered painfully. It was taking away the numbness he had felt since he had gotten the phone call. It had been comforting, a wall of protection from the feelings and emotions that threatened to overwhelm him. Her presence brought a different sort of comfort though, the first glimpse that there was something beyond those crushing, overwhelming emotions. Her presence offered hope.

When the service was over, Ian sat there while a parade of people offered condolences. When the line had wound down Brian approached and offered to drive him home.

"Actually, I think Breezy here is going to take me, right?"

She nodded her acceptance to the plan and they made their way out to the car. Their hands separating only because Symone need it for driving, the drive home passed silently. They walked into his apartment and Symone's eyes immediately landed on a blank piece of wall that had used to hold a picture he had taken, the evidence of its previous existence being alluded to by an indent in the wall made by the frame.

"Yeah I had a little accident with some glass."

"I heard about your little tantrum. I understand the coffee maker is no more. A coffee run will be in order. I'm sweating in all this black though; can I use your shower? Is there a mirror left in there?"

That earned her a snigger. "Of course, heaven forbid I can't see to right my hair."

"Of course, heaven forbid."

She took her shower and he changed into sweats. All of a sudden he didn't have the energy to even keep open his eyes so he lay down on his bed and listened to the steady sound of the shower. She stepped out of the bathroom and quietly walked over to the bed.

"I'm not asleep."

"Maybe you should be" as she extended a hip to sit on the edge of the bed.

"I could sleep for days and it wouldn't help," was his brusque rejoinder.

"What would help?"

"I don't know. You got a time machine on you?"

"I've got the next best thing. Tell me what regrets you would go back and change?"

"It is too long of a list." His pointed stare conveying without words the regrets he had involved her?

"Ok, how about just regrets concerning Jace."

"Ah, well that's easy. I would have been with him the night he died. He said he didn't need me, and obviously he was wrong?"

"Since I know you won't believe it isn't your fault; I'll ask what you would have done to protect him."

"I would have had him in a cab; he wouldn't have been on the streets."

"And if they found you to together, you might have been killed instead."

Good, at least he would be alive."

She stretched out beside him on the bed and replied, "Really? You would have him here; inflict this pain you are feeling on him? Worse actually, cause he would have to live with being the cause of his brother's death."

Those words hung in the air and the only response that came was for him to turn and busy his head in her shoulder while he wept. She held him while he wept. They stayed in that pose until the grief left energy for nothing else but sleep.

The next morning saw Symone alerting work she would in late. She would be in late because Ian insisted she not miss work on his account. After extracting promises from Brian that he would check in during the day she finally headed into work. It was a productive day even if she did call and check in on Ian every hour or two. He threatened to not answer the phone but was secretly glad to hear her voice each time. She didn't spend the night but the checking in repeated every day for the first week, and once a week the month to follow. She didn't ask if he was feeling better and he didn't ask her to stop calling. It was an unspoken agreement they both could live with.

Symone was at home thinking of calling Ian to check on him when her phone rang:

"Hey Mom" she feigned excitement.

"Symone, honey. I need to tell you something. Are your sisters with you by chance?"

"No, what is it?"

"Your dad honey... he died this morning" she got out between sobs.

Because Symone couldn't get anything out between the nausea in her stomach and horrible lump in her throat, she just asked how he died. She was told that he had developed leukemia, and they found it at such a late stage treatments didn't help. He hadn't suffered long, he had been made comfortable.

Symone spent the night with her sisters, Raven and her both at Kat's. The next day since Kat was being comforted by Brian and Raven was napping she went home to take a shower and call work. She had just stepped out of the shower when the doorbell rang. Thinking that Raven had tracked her down, she opened the door in frustration:

"I was coming back . . ." she paused when Ian stretched out his arms. She flew into them so forcefully it was as if that used up the back of her strength. Her legs went out from under her, and Ian's embrace the only thing holding her up.

He carried her to the sofa and positioned them so she could lay her head in his lap.

LOVE HOPES ALL THINGS

"I think he tried to tell me he was sick. He asked me to visit; maybe he would have told me
I had gone. Why didn't I go?" she sobbed as she leaned into him.

"He knew you loved him, Symone" to which she sighed and a tenseness in her body loosened.
He attempted to further that progress by slowly stroking her face and was rewarded with a
soft purr of a moan in response.

"So, when are you going down to Mexico?"

"I'm not, at least not right away. Kat and Raven are, but he's being cremated so we'll do a
celebration of life in a few months. I just can't go right now, I feel and probably sound selfish
thinking this way and I do love Kathy but my sister's have their mother still, while I . . .I feel
like . . . I am an orphan."

"As a fellow orphan I can assure you, you don't sound selfish." To which she responded by
looking up at him, smiling, and cupping his cheek in her hand.

When grief and the comfort of a friend had both expended her energy and lulled her to sleep
he picked her up and put her to bed. He curled up beside her and offered the comfort of his
presence, wishing it could compare to the peace her presence brought him.

Symone awoke to the pleasant feeling of warmth and realized it was the body heat of the
person beside her.

"Good morning" she said when he stirred.

"Good morning, I have to say your bed may be bigger but I think mine is more comfortable,"
which didn't really require a response.

Faced with the novelty of not having to report to work Symone suggested they do something
frivolous and fun. In response, a trip to the very spot they met was proposed. Although both
were in agreement that no capture-the-flag was to be played the idea was unanimously
agreed upon. Preparations were made, bags were packed. Symone phoned Raven and told
her of her plans lest they worry about her whilst she was out of cell phone range.

The trip up the mountain seemed to pass in a blur and not just because Ian drove with a lead
foot. Symone stepped out of the car and closed her eyes as the sun and fresh air washed over
her and went an incredible way to buoying her spirits. They completed the hike and made
camp in no time. The trip would be marked by the most remarkable companionable silence
ever. Whether it was reading with the head of one on the lap of the other, hiking toward a
waterfall, or making a meal neither one really had the appetite to eat it was as if words were
not necessary. Not to say they didn't have conversation because they did but it didn't
compare to the comfort that went unspoken. The weather cooperated nicely, as if it sensed

that both campers needed the respite. All too soon the trip was over and they headed back both significantly rejuvenated enough to go back to everyday life. Ian dropped Symone off, had helped her in with her bags and was leaving when Symone stood on tip toe and caressed his neck

"I had such a nice week, thank you for proposing it."

"Thank you for being delightful company" he responded. To which she scoffed.

He started down the driveway and turned and said:

"I know you'll be with family, but if you want company when you go to Mexico let me know."

"I will. Thanks"

Chapter 7 – A New Life

However, when time came for Symone to go to Mexico, she was so pre-occupied that not only did she not think about inviting Ian it had not even occurred to her that they hadn't talked recently. Part of that could be attributed to her constant state of exhaustion. She looked at her face in the mirror while she was waiting for her sisters to pick her for the airport and promptly decided to add some more concealer around the eyes. She dismissed it as grief and assured herself this week would rejuvenate her and so it wouldn't do to worry anyone.

The celebration was beautiful and dignified and it was wonderful to be with family and share their memories of her dad. They laughed, cried, and told stories while they worked on sorting through his belongings. However, a part of her couldn't help but want to be alone, alone with her grief and memories of her dad before her mom died, memories that were hers alone.

Sunning by the pool or on the beach allowed her that solitude. It was one such time she had availed her of when Kathy approached her:

"May I join you?"

"You don't have to ask mom."

"I didn't want to disturb your solitude but I wanted to do this while your sisters were out. I have something for you" and she held out a box.

Symone opened the box and in it was the most beautiful locket on the most delicate chain she could have imagined. She fingered the latch on the locket to open it and gasped while her hand went to her mouth.

"Oh Kathy I don't know what to say."

"Your father had this saved with the picture of your mother for you. I added his picture just recently"

"Thank you so much, I love it"

"Good, now can an old lady express some concern without getting lip in return?"

Symone stifled a laugh. The lady was a force to be reckoned with, no doubt about it. She would have had to be to put up with her dad. Symone nodded her assent

"You are way too skinny and frail looking, dear. If you don't start taking care of yourself I'm going to have to lock you in your room until such times things change."

When seeing the surprise on Symone's face she continued:

"Did you really think you're fooling anyone with those loose shirts, makeup and sunglasses?"

"I have been tired; I guess it's the stress. I will take better care of myself I promise."

"That includes going to the doctor when you get home young lady."

"Ok, I will"

"Just because that's not my picture in that locket doesn't mean I don't care about you as if you were my own," she said with the slightest hint of a sniffle

"I know. I love you mom. You have always been wonderful to me" she said as she hugged Kathy

"I'll leave you be now, just mind you keep me informed about your doctor's appointment. I'll send your little sisters after you if you don't."

Symone giggled as the woman walked away.

She caught a different flight home than Raven and Kat because she wanted to set some plans in motion before she had to work. Whether it was the loss of her dad or the warmth of her family she had made a decision to have a family of her own. Since she had no intentions on marrying and she loved the idea of giving love to an unwanted child so she had made an appointment at an adoption agency.

In fact, the idea excited her so much she had forgotten about the promise she had made Kathy, to see the doctor, until the agency requested she have a medical exam as part of the process. So she found herself in the doctor's office when a tall, broad shouldered, good looking man walked in the room.

"Hi I'm Dr. Nichols; I see you're the agency sent you here. Tell me about yourself, health, appetite."

"I don't seem to have much energy or appetite lately. I recently lost my father though so I figure that's why"

"I'm very sorry for your loss. Tell me any weight loss?"

"Some," was her casual response.

"Actually" he said, flipping through notes "since you were seen three months ago you've lost 20 pounds. I'd like to run some blood work"

Symone got the lab work done and thought no more of her doctor's appointment, focused as she was on the adoption. She was interviewed by several couples, filled out endless reams of paperwork, and went through the home inspection. Her respite from having to go through all the hoops and red tape was setting up the nursery, buying baby things. She didn't allow herself to buy clothes because she wasn't sure if her child would be a boy or a girl. Her sisters even got excite for her, discussing plans for a baby shower whenever she got final news from the adoption agency. Anxious as she was to hear from the adoption agency when the phone rang she expected it to be them:

"Hello"

"Hello, this is Dr. Nichols. Is this Symone, Miss Watkins?"

"It is"

"I have news on your blood work, when are you available to come into the office to discuss them"

"Oh um, it is my day off so I can come in today."

"Good, the front desk will be expecting you."

As she sat in the office awaiting the doctor it struck her that the office and the furnishings were almost as handsome as the occupant. The place smelled of him too. It had been a long time since she had appreciated a good looking man. Ian's face came into her mind. This reverie was interrupted by the entrance of Dr. Nichols:

"Thank you for coming in. I will get right down to it. Unfortunately, your blood work showed evidence of osteosarcoma"

"I'm sorry what?"

"Osteosarcoma, it's a form of cancer that attacks the bones."

"Am I going to die?" she dropped the hands that had shot up to her mouth at hearing the news down to the desk. Dr. Nichols reached over and covered them with his palm.

We won't know more until we do more tests. What stage, or how advanced it is. Some are more aggressive than others. Everybody responds to treatment differently. May I ask what kind of support system you have?"

"Two very devoted sisters"

"Good, here is my private number if you or your sisters have any questions. Next steps, we need to get you a PET scan and we'll decide the best treatment protocol when we have those results."

They made her next appointment and she left. She drove home without knowing how she got there, the fog and haze from the news she'd just received not having cleared yet. Somewhere through the fog she heard the phone ring again:

"Hello, this is Ruby from the Adoption Agency. I'm afraid I have some bad news"

"More bad news" went through Symone's mind but somehow didn't come out her mouth. On hearing the silence the lady from the adoption agency proceeded.

"I am afraid the baby we told you about is no longer available. When the parents heard what a closed adoption meant they changed their mind. I don't want you to lose heart; this process takes some time in most cases.

Symone vaguely remembered responding and giving the normal courtesies to end the conversation and sat down on her couch. Symone would call it their dinner plans; Raven would call it 'sisterly intuition'. Whatever the case she appeared at the exact moment she was needed and proceeded to be a god-send from then on.

They discussed the news about her health, completely relegating the adoption to non-importance. Kathy and Kat were informed and it took all three sisters to convince Kathy not to move there to help care for Symone. Amidst much badgering Symone firmly held that she would continue working until after the PET scan. Raven and Symone had talked about becoming roommates after Kat's wedding and now that became a certainty.

A combination of radiation and chemo was decided upon and life turned into and endless line of doctor's appointments even with the at home d-i-y chemo machine. To say that Symone look back on this point in her life with fondness may seem weird but she would. If anything, the bond between her and Raven grew closer, they made a joke of the hair loss, watched girlie movies, gave pedicures and all other sorts of creature comforts. At times, Kat was a break away from married life and join them and then the sibling camaraderie was truly complete. They were so focused on her comfort; Symone had to worry Raven getting 'caregiver burn-out' which surely would have happened if Kat hadn't been around to give her a break. Even Brian would bring flowers or hold her after a nasty bout of nausea from the chemo. It was during one such low point she looked at her locket and came to the realization she was not alone.

Six months later . . .

Symone was sleeping off the effects of the latest dose of treatment when she opened her eyes because of the soft touch of someone holding her hand. When she opened them, instead of Raven as she expected; there was quite a different person by her bed.

"Hey stranger" she said as she squeezed his hand.

"Didn't expect to see me did you?"

"Honestly no. I thought you were Raven and I was going to scold her for returning early, she supposed to take the day off."

"What a selfless patient"

"More like demanding and cranky patient," she said with a giggle. "Kat is gone I take it."

"Yes, I'm afraid I sent her home to Brian, told her I could undertake care of you in the meantime"

It was at that exact moment Symone got an attack of nausea and wave of pain from the treatments. After she was done getting sick he helped her back to bed and got her some pain medicine and water to wash it down. He patted the perspiration from her forehead with a damp cloth.

"Why are you here, Ian?" she said with eyes so pleading and voice so weak it tore at his heart.

"Honestly, because I want to be. I know our relationship has been rocky and know you wanted space but when I heard you were ill I just thought there must be a way to get past all the nonsense in my head. I have made you feel that I don't love you but it simply isn't true. I love you so dearly. When I think of the time that has been wasted. . ."

"So let's not waste anymore dwelling on regrets."

Any further conversation was interrupted by Raven entering the house.

"Hey honey I'm home. Whose stuff is that in the spare room?" she stopped when she saw that her sister had a visitor. "Hey Ian" she greeted less than cheerfully.

Symone glared at her sister and then looked at Ian and realized that a tacit agreement that he was staying existed. Raven announced she was retiring to her end of the house and they didn't see any more of her for the night

Ian pulled a comfortable chair up to the side of the bed and graciously offered her the choice of entertainment for the evening.

"Are you sure you know what you're getting yourself into."

"I'll risk it."

After much teasing her about acceding to sick people she retaliated by smacking him with a pillow and picking a chick flick as her choice of entertainment. When the movie was over he noticed the beads of sweat on her forehead and that she had a slight shiver. It was time for medication and after she indicated by name which medication she needed he quickly retrieved it for her. He wasn't sure which bothered him most the large volume of pills she apparently took or her pallor and obvious discomfort. When he asked what else he could do for her comfort she indicated that the pain medication just needed to take effect and that she would be fine. The shiver hadn't left her body so he slowly climbed into bed with her.

"This is definitely not your king size."

"No but it takes the burden to be flexible off me," and she blushed at her own innuendo.

"Naughty girl" he said as he nuzzled her cheek and pulled her closer.

Soon the sounds of each other's breathing lulled both to sleep. This is the scene that Raven came in on when she went to check on her dear sister in the morning. When Ian came in to collect a cup of coffee for Symone he was met with the pique of a protective sister.

"Ian, I have nothing against you. She's dying though and the last thing she needs is you messing with her head or whatever drama goes on with you two. She needs to be left in peace."

"Raven, I totally agree with you, I am here for the long haul. If I wasn't I promise I would not have come. I absolutely adore that you are protective of her. We are on the same team; we both have her best interests at heart."

Raven decided time would tell and she would not be disappointed. Ian stayed by her sister's side. He worked at her side, deciding to do a project that allowing him time free of travel. He read to her, and he made sure she took her meds. It was no longer shocking for Raven to walk in and find Ian helping with leg exercises that helped avoid muscle atrophy. However, mostly they talked. They talked about everything. One day Symone was telling him about the plans she had had for adoption and he asked if she had any names picked out for the baby when he was interrupted:

"How is my favorite patient today?" greeted Dr. Nichols

"Do you want the truth?" Symone cynically responded.

"Am I to take that as indication that it is a bad day?" the handsome doctor smiled which checking her pulse.

"Nah. That was me being silly. You didn't know I was a comedian?"

"Humor is a good sign, indication that you are getting good care" he gave Ian a fleeting glance. "Any medications need re-filled."

"I doubt it. Raven wouldn't let them get low. She would know for sure."

"Actually Dr., I noticed the pain medication seems to be getting low," Ian chimed in.

"Well, I think I'm creating a monster, but I'll refill it" he gave a cheeky wink and smile to Symone and left. He had no sooner left the room than,

"I see, so all this is for attention from Dr. Hottie?" Ian asked with the biggest smirk on his face.

"I'm not even going to dignify that with a response but Dr. Hottie? Really? That is ridiculous" she emphasized by poking him in the ribs

"Ok, Ok I give I give. As long as you admit that you have a crush on Dr. Hottie" he said as he left the room to dodge the pillow being tossed at him.

Later when she was worn out and having a reaction the treatment she realized how important that levity was to her well-being. It even affected Raven, because instead of having a crease in her forehead from worry lines and furrowed brows she looked more at ease and had even gone back to work. For Symone herself, the benefit was less tangible. Her response to treatment was still less than encouraging and she still dealt with the side effects of the treatment but his presence made it all more bearable. No better example of this was there than the one night he came out of the shower with his head shaved. Symone saw him and couldn't stop laughing.

"Why in the world did you do that?"

"It looks so good on you I couldn't help myself; I had to be like you. I think it will be a thing"

"Yeah you think so, scarf and all?" she said as she pulled him to her side and kissed his cheek.

"Scarf makes it; I'm all depressed I can't find one for me"

"Shut Up" she said and laid her head on the shoulder she just smacked.

"So what did you want to name the baby you were going to adopt?"

"That's random but I happened to have given that a lot of thought. I wanted Sophie for a girl and Ethan for a boy."

"Not random at all, Dr. Hottie interrupted me asking the other day and I like those names."

He thought of the empty nursery next door and tried to swallow down the lump in his throat. The heaviness in his heart wasn't so easily dismissed. He thought about how much Symone wanted to be a mother and what a good one she would be. That such child wouldn't know the wealth of love she could give and it broke his heart. Thinking oh her no longer being in his life was unfathomable. He responded by getting in bed beside her and she wasted no time in curling up into his chest.

"Shall we watch a movie?" he asked as he kissed and stroked her hair.

"As long as neither of us has to get up to turn it on" she purred, not willing to relinquish her comfortable pillow.

Coincidentally, Raven came home and popped her head in to check in on her sister and obliged them by starting the movie for them. She smiled and didn't make the snide comment that crossed her mind about Ian sitting through Pride and Prejudice for her sister. She was just glad to see how happy the both of them seemed during these trying circumstances.

Hours later with the slight sound of television in the background Ian and Symone slept in each other's arms. Symone had been lulled to sleep by the sound of his heart, and him by the soft sound of her breathing. This was the scene that greeted Raven in the morning when she brought Symone her coffee and morning medicine. When Symone didn't respond when she tried to rouse her she let out a whimper of grief but when she looked over and saw Ian's face crumpled in grief she knew she had to be strong.

The next day Raven was over at Kat's and Ian was on the couch dazing into space, lost in thoughts and memories when a knock on the door disturbed him. He went to the door and a woman in a business suit was there, smile on her face, with a baby in her arms.

"Is Symone Watkins here?"

Ian somehow explained that she had passed away and the lady then described that this was the child Symone wanted to adopt and that since the last attempt fell through she didn't have much contact with Symone and hadn't heard she had been ill.

Finally realizing the baby in the social worker's arms, Ian took her from the social worker and looked in her face. Her dark hair was in stark contrast to her porcelain skin and she was wearing a ruffled green dress and bow that were fit for a princess, and then the baby opened her eyes and wrapped her hand around his finger. . .

Epilogue

Ian looked in the mirror and groaned the way he always did when he was heading to an event he would rather not be at.

It had been a year but still not a day went by without her being in his thoughts. A few months after her death Symone's sister's had tried to play matchmaker for him as if he was some widower that needed to move on after losing his partner in life. However, Symone hadn't been his wife, he wasn't a widower and he didn't deserve their comfort. He sighed, he needed to go. Kat and Raven had become like sisters to him and it wouldn't do to make them worry by begging off.

"Let's go Sofie."

A little bundle of bouncing brunette waves and dark, sparkling eyes ran into the room.

"I'm ready Daddy," as she ran into his arms. She squealed when he tickled and bestowed kisses all over her cheeks.

They pulled up to Kat and Brian's and after appropriate fawning over Sofie they greeted Ian as well. The apartment was crowded with friends and at first Ian couldn't enjoy himself because Sofie would get out of eye sight and he got very nervous when that happened. Raven came walking towards him with Sofie in her arms, and he breathed a little easier.

"There, Daddy see's you're ok and he isn't scowling and scaring the guests any longer."

"I guess I am a little overprotective" he half smiled at Raven while taking Sofie in her arms.

"Just a little?" she asked.

He responded with a scowl and she winked in response. She was so different from Symone and yet slightly reminiscent. No matter what, it was hard to be anything but grateful to two uch doting and devoted aunties. Sofie, safely restored to her father squirmed in his arms not aving the nervous compunction to separation that he did.

Ok you wiggle worm, stay close."

his time she ran to her aunt Kat and when he could see her safely ensconced there he elaxed. A cute blonde suddenly attached herself to his arm. He was looking at her in disbelief for her presumptuousness when he suddenly recognized her as someone who used to pend a lot of time with his brother. While his brother's memory was also precious to him, he days of partying with him wasn't how he wanted to remember him.

omehow he made it through the night. Guests were saying their good bye and he had to admit he had enjoyed himself. He had gotten to catch up with Brian. He got to tease Brian mercilessly when they had announced they were expecting a baby. Kat glanced in his direction and they shared a glassy eyed knowing glance for their loved one who couldn't share he moment with them.

ofie was the center of attraction, which was no surprise. That kind of attention takes a lot out of a person so the end of the night saw her asleep on Uncle Brian's shoulder. Ian went to collect her and was intercepted by Raven who said she had something for him. When he opened it his breath hitched when he saw that it was a picture frame with a picture of ymone on one and her poem of hope on the other.

As he was putting Sofie to bed she woke up and asked who it was, he answered:

Your mom"

Will you tell me about her?"

As he bent to kiss her he got a whiff of ocean and smiled

You bet Breezy" he said with a smile and kissed her forehead. "You bet."